Sword in the Darkness

Sword in the Darkness

PAOLO BICCHIERI

RESOURCE *Publications* · Eugene, Oregon

Resource Publications
An Imprint of Wipf and Stock Publishers
199 W. 8th Ave., Suite 3
Eugene, OR 97401

www.wipfandstock.com

PAPERBACK ISBN: 978-1-7252-5161-8
HARDCOVER ISBN: 978-1-7252-5162-5
EBOOK ISBN: 978-1-7252-5163-2

Manufactured in the U.S.A.   04/18/19

Dedicated to the Native people of the West Coast
who resist by existing.

"We are the ones we've been waiting for,"

–June Jordan

Contents

Acknowledgments

This book is possible only through the support and love I receive from my Nonno, Nonna, Grandma Floy, Grandpa Bill, Grandma Sherrie, Grandpa Dale, Abuela, and Chacon. The same is true for the joy and wisdom given by Luca, Sage, Clairey, Teo, and Davey Pecos Bill. And, still, my mom and my dad.

Thanks to the inspiration from the folks at the Creative Writing Institute of Martha's Vineyard, the Grotto, the panelists from 2019's AWP in Portland, Quiet Lightning, and all my writing mentors.

Thank you to 826 Valencia and the wonderful, talented, patient people doing the work of amplifying young people's voices through writing.

And to all the people I love and who have loved me on the West Coast. I love you and am thinking about you.

Prologue

THE WOODS WERE HIGH, and children ran amongst them like fish swimming up river. As fish leap through the crested creeks, the children splashed from tree to tree, their faces painted with happy moments.

Each chose their own spot as they saw fit—floating from branch to branch and dashing from trunk to trunk. Their families strode along with them.

The Winahl River was alive with their people. Shouts and happy voices were thrown around like a twice-told tale. The travelers were coming back to their loamy Klamath lands after a council held for all of the Kalapuyan speaking natives at the powerful, churning river basin.

Their huts had thatched arms outstretched to receive. Scattered and few, their homes were just as powerful as the people—resilient. Resistant.

But new faces were in their homes when they returned. White men with their odd clothes and great tools were dotted around their familiar home.

A Klamath man, tall with a body like a scarecrow, found a friendly face.

"Who are these people?"

"Settlers. Didn't they take speak of them at the council?"

"Yes, but there was no mention of their coming in toward the plains. I thought they'd stick to the waters they've *already* taken."

His friend simply shrugged and walked away. It was an unhappy conversation to have, they both knew that. It was the unhappy conversation of the status of their freedom. The man with the foxy eyes knew that, but he wasn't about to worry his people. Not yet.

He walked into the woods and spoke with the people of the woods, the boqs. They yelled and hooted but couldn't see any threat from the strangers. The Klamath native growled that there *will* be a problem. That they will bring with them plunder. That they will bring with them secrets. That they will bring with them ancient rites that just might stick around.

The boqs were too open-minded, too honest. The man walked back to the village. It was a long walk, but he had a long gait.

As he walked the path back toward the Klamath home, there was a big cave that opened on the side of the trail. He was puzzled—there was certainly no cave there when he left. Caves were dark and spelunky things, but the tall fellow walked in nonetheless.

There was a dim light coming from somewhere back and beyond. His feet raised and fell like keys to a piano, gentle and quiet. Big spikes rose from the floor of the cave and sometimes bigger spikes drooled from the ceiling.

For a man like him it was no trouble to find his way through the cave. He knew the natural world and its labyrinths better than almost any, except maybe his brother Blu-Jay. But he was a King, after all.

Toward the end it became like a mine for a moment, but only from one stone. One stone placed inside the face of a tremendously impressive item the man had never seen before. It stood with a curve in its upright position like a bent and unbroken tree. The base of the thing grew from a mound of broken dirt.

"My god," a voice came from behind the native.

The man spun around to see one of the White invaders. He narrowed his eyes and told the intruder that he had made the discovery—that it was his to judge.

"I-I'm sorry, I don't speak. . .I just saw the sword is all," the man raised his hands like a good churchgoing man should.

The black haired man shook his head slowly, then walked toward the sword. "Sword" sounded funny to him, but there was nothing funny about the thing itself. He took a hand and ran it alongside its long side.

"Oh don't do –"

Blood dripped from his fingers. The man studied his hand for a moment. Then as quickly as it had been cut it was healed. The White man watching dropped his shovel, something he would have not needed in this place.

This time grabbing the base of the thing, the man placed his hands upon it and, like people have always done, tried to rip it from its prison. It was no good.

"Here," the White man said. "Maybe I'll try?"

The Klamath man smiled a big smile. His grip on the sword only tightened, and the White man took a few steps toward the mouth of the cave. His eyes turned a faint yellow. As they did, a pressure built in the cave. The man's handsome black hair tore around his head like a cyclone. His eyes glossed a pristine white rather than the ambient yellow from before.

Earth toppled away from the sword. It was as though it had been awakened. Someone pulled the shades up on the dingy bedroom of the cave. As it rose, the stone in its blade glimmered like a fantastic treasure.

"My god," the White man was like a sick parrot. "Just, wow."

"It is a powerful and old thing," the man said. "Shall we try it out?"

The White man now dropped his lantern. It broke into tiny memories.

"You speak English?"

"Don't be so surprised," the man said. "It's an ugly thing for your kind to be so surprised. But you seem nice enough, stranger. What's your name?"

"Thomas Rightmore," he mumbled. "I'm just –"

"Let's find our way out of here, Thomas. Let's have a look at this sword."

The two spoke of many things as they back trailed their way out of the cave. It was so fascinating for Thomas, so melancholy for the Klamath man. Both wanted to share their worlds, but instead found themselves talking about this sword. It illuminated their path so that they wouldn't fall into dark traps in the cave.

Back on the path outside the cave, they finally saw it for what it was—a miracle given from the earth. Gaea's bounty given shape.

The Klamath man took the sword again and focused his will. The effect was breathtaking. Birds took to the sky in the hundreds, right out of thin air. Bison rampaged on either side of the two men, but only ran a few feet before tumbling back into the aether again. Big sunflowers sprouted under their feet then receded into seeds once more.

"I'd like to try," the White man said. "If it's alright."

The black haired man furrowed his brow.

"Of course it isn't," he said. "Why would I let some unfamiliar trespasser like yourself tinker with some unfamiliar tool in *my* lands?"

The White man shifted his weight, casting his eyes to the ground. He murmured, then began to walk toward the Klamath Native, swinging his arms like a baboon.

"Hold on, now," the Klamath man whispered.

The looming pale body was upon the Klamath, swinging arms arcing down toward his shoulders, when power consumed the area again. Thomas was thrown to the ground as a dome of light, like little motes of sunset, grew from the Klamath man. The sword had remained quiet in his hands. Thomas sat up, and the Native stared at him with eyes of yellow stone.

"Do not try that again, Thomas," he spoke. "It would be your last mistake."

"Ah," Thomas looked at the sword again as he rose. "You'd best not give it to me after all. Truth be told I worry what my folk and I coming here does for a place like this at all. My wife and boy sure do like it here, but I wouldn't want to impose any further than we might be already."

The Klamath man's big smile returned to his face, knowing and long like the gorge he lived upon.

"You *may* be right, Thomas," the man said. "We'd best be rid of the thing. It would be a shame for any, you know, *trespassers* to get ahold of it."

Thomas scratched his chin for a second, then smiled. The two walked down the path and toward the Klamath homes. The cave sat stoically along the path, as foreign as Thomas and his people. A stony wart.

After they traced their way through the woods and were just outside the village, they dug a great well, the Klamath moving most of the dirt. They had chatted the whole way, though Thomas was flabbergasted that a Klamath man could speak *his* language.

The well fell straight down, like the edge of the world. The White man looked to the local.

"What do you think?"

The Klamath man peered down the long shaft. His eyes flickered yellow, and the hole deepened even further, cracking into the planet. Thomas came up just behind him.

"I think –"

A foolish punch cut him off. Thomas rubbed his hand as the man twirled to the ground. Thomas caught the sword by the hilt. He rose it above his head like it was the hands of a clock striking midnight.

"Your gluttonous eyes have erased your memory, Thomas," the Klamath spoke.

A pool of ambient light again flourished from where the man lay and Thomas flew backward. He pin-wheeled his arms, teetered, then sank into the pit he had barely helped to make. Simply orchestrated.

"Never trust a nice guy," the Klamath mumbled, rising from where he lay.

He picked up the sword and admired the blade's gorgeous jewel. A sigh escaping his cracked lips, he tossed the alien tool to sink through the fresh air. His long black hair pranced in the cool air as he watched it sail away and below.

He didn't think of what the sword wanted, though, or of who else besides a colonist may hope to wield the sword in the darkness.

Chapter 1

OAKLAND, CALIFORNIA, IS NOT as sunny as one might think. It can be foggy like the clouds just won't budge for anything. In October and November is when it's sunniest.

Marisol Puentes didn't care for Oakland. She didn't care for much outside of a few simple things. Those simple things made the other things worth putting up with, but everyone has their limit. And she had reached hers.

"Drew Barrymore" by SZA hummed from her phone. She slapped the phone as fast as she could and turned it off before her brothers woke up.

But, just like every other day, up popped Tomas. Her youngest brother at six-years-old, Tomas had eyes full of the kind of magic one finds in a Pixar movie, bright and unafraid.

"Good morning Mary-sol," he whispered. "Don't wake up Carlicito because if you do he will spit on you."

"I don't think that's true," Marisol whispered. "But it's *you* who's being loud, hermanito."

Tomas' mouth opened in the widest O, so embarrassed that he hadn't realized it first, and he scampered out of the room. His feet sounded like the pads of a puppy against the hardwood floor.

She slid off the top bunk and down to the hardwood below. None of the remaining five brothers stirred at all.

"Buenas dias, mija," her mom said to her when she came out. The house was colorful and wonderful, but she saw her father reading his laptop at the table. Tomas sat in the front room smashing a lamb and a Paw

Patrol action figure together. Her father's coffee steamed, and he looked even hotter.

"Este presidente, god this whole country," he spat. "If it wasn't for us, who would trim your precious White House lawn, heh? Dios *mio*."

"Try to relax, Santos."

Her parents came to California when California came to Mexico—the Puentes were Americanized without consent in 1848. Her padre was terribly proud of that, and her mother was, too. She showed her pride by being an excellent madre, but her father showed it by being kind of rude to everyone who wasn't Mexican.

"Ay, I'm so upset, Lutecia," he slapped the paper down. "I'm going out tonight with some guys from work. We have work to do."

Marisol couldn't really blame him. But it still hurt her to see things so embroiled in rejection. And going out with "some guys" usually resulted in a hard next day for her mom. She wanted to be left alone with tierra and her computer. Those two things gave her all the control she wanted.

"Los primos are outside," Lutecia said as she pushed a Go-Gurt into a brown bag. "Here you go, Marisol. Te amo mucho."

"I love you, too, mom," Marisol said as she grabbed the bag. Three of her brothers, Ernesto, Louis, and Jorge, all flung free from their room. Somehow they had dressed themselves and gotten ready to leave in a few short minutes. Marisol was so taken aback each day that though she was up the earliest and most prepared, she was the last one out the door.

The fog kept things coastal. Mexico this was not, anymore, even though seeing her cousins stocked in a beater Toyota Tacoma like toothpicks in a jar might have confused some. Four in the cab, and three in the bed. She jumped in the bed with her brothers.

"Hola," Marisol said. "Any word from Carlo?"

"Nada," said her cousin, Benecio.

It was harder than ever to be a Puentes, she thought. As the truck rolled over potholes and bumped her around like a bag of chicken feed, she thought about revolutions, about Zapata and Chavez. About the freedom and independence to decide where to go and when to go there. About the only revolutionary things she would do today—art and coding.

The flags on the flagpole were at their full height today, but she thought they should have been at half-mast for quite a while now. Five of them got out at Baldwin High, with the rest unloading at Verdant Oaks Elementary, backpacks cinched. No one wanted their stuff taken.

She went to the bathroom to get ready for the day—since her cousins came so early, she always ducked into the school bathroom to make sure she didn't invite any extra attention.

Her thick rim glasses made her look like an old reporter for an old newspaper. She wished she had contacts, or at least glasses that had an up-to-date prescription, but neither were in the cards. At least the color matched her long hair.

It wasn't a big school, but it really didn't need to be. Each kid still had their own locker, so you could tell that kids were being taken care of. Marisol had a half-hour until her Language Arts, the *English* language, class began. So she dashed her backpack in her locker and went to the art room.

Mrs. Neuschwander was in her room as always, short yellow hair and emerald eyes ablaze. The kiln helped with that.

"Marisol! Good morning!"

"Good morning, Mrs. N," Marisol said. "Would it be okay if-"

"You don't have to ask every day, you know. I'm *glad* some students want to use the facility before class."

Mrs. Neuschwander turned to the cabinets above the kiln as Marisol stood on tip-toes behind her. The Ms. Frizzle-inspired teacher turned around and gave Marisol a brick of clay.

"Have at it!"

"Gracias," Marisol whispered. "I think I'll make a sunflower."

"That's wonderful, Marisol. I'll be at my desk if you need me."

Mrs. Neuschwander had been in trouble when Marisol was in seventh grade. She had made a lot of ruckus about one of the other teachers, Mr. Dackerson, and how he was talking inappropriately to his co-workers. Everyone was upset with her, and even the paper talked about her, but in the end they found out that Mr. Dackerson really *had* been saying and doing all kinds of not-okay things.

Now that Marisol was 16-years-old she really admired Mrs. N. She considered herself extra lucky that Mrs. N also happened to be the art teacher. When she wanted to come make some art, she also got to hang out with one of her biggest role models. For all the times that her dad wasn't okay to her mom, and said things that were really out of line, she thought about how Mrs. Neuschwander would put him in his place.

Marisol stood near the kiln, some heat radiating in her mind, and worked the brick into a ball. She started to roll it out from there into what she imagined would be the stem of her flower. She wet her hands a bit and kept molding, making some petals and laying them on a paper towel.

She'd have to wait to bake it, but if she worked hard before class, maybe she'd be ready to bake by the end of fifth period, when she was actually *supposed* to be in Mrs. Neuschwander's room.

The warning bell dinged its droning prophecy. Marisol looked at how much there was to put away, and Mrs. Neuschwander told her to just leave it behind the sink for fifth period.

"Thanks for letting me come by this morning, Mrs. N," Marisol said.

"Don't thank me, and speak up a little, Marisol," she replied from her desk. "You don't need to be so quiet. You're one of the most talented kids *at* Baldwin."

"Oh, thank you, Mrs. N," she said. She buttoned up her multi-colored fleece that, though it was a hot day, felt good to have clamped all the way up to her chin.

After vocab quizzes and silent reading was behind her, and a couple of classes about someone else's history, and the most alien language of all, Algebra, she got to fourth period: computer science.

There were a couple of ways Marisol loved to create, but they were all with her hands.

"Sit down, and boot up your computers," Mr. Balzoni said as kids filed in. "They're no Windows Vista, am I right kids? Ha."

The computers hummed to life as the kids chattered about each other, mostly. Marisol talked to her friend Nina about the flower she was working on—how excited she'd be when it was cast with the right paint.

"Go ahead and work on assignment 3.1 from HTML," Mr. Balzoni continued. "HTML Yes! The Pun-loving Guide to Coding" was some jokester's idea of sprucing up the stereotypically un-fun world of coding. But puns or not, Marisol loved it.

Sitting through a class not made for her was as fun as riding in the bed of her Uncle Felipe's cruddy truck. Trying to navigate a system designed to keep people with her heritage "in their place" was even less fun. But making flowers and learning how the internet worked, how the *internet worked!*, made it all worth-while.

Until today.

Even Marisol had a limit. People couldn't tell, because she kept things together as well as she did. But there was a limit.

She was so excited when Mrs. Neuschwander's class came around. She had been waiting all day to keep working on her sunflower. But as soon as she opened the door she could tell something was wrong.

"Hey Mrs. N," Marisol whispered, noticing a few kids standing at the back of the room.

"Oh, Marisol, let me talk to you in the hall for a minute," she said, an arm stretched out in a plea. She began to walk toward Marisol, but Marisol had already put her bag down and was making her way to the back of the room.

She wiggled through a couple of taller boys and one shorter boy. They circled around the sink like coyotes. All of them were giggling and telling each other to "shut up, dude."

Her flower was smooshed, ruined. Each pedal had been pinned to the wall above the flower, with the now goopified stem below. A pink sticky note was taped to the gooseneck faucet that read:

"Go home, beaner!"

She felt a lump fall from her throat to her stomach. It was about the size of her heart.

"Um," Marisol quivered.

"Let's go in the hall, Marisol," Mrs. Neuschwander said. "Some boys were jealous of your creation, that's all."

She lay a hand on Marisol's shoulder, but Marisol shrugged it off, slow like it didn't hurt.

"I had better go," Marisol said. She walked as fast as one can go while still walking, grabbed her backpack, and left the room. She wanted to go sit in front of her locker to cry, at least for a little bit. Then she made her mind up.

She didn't notice the tears in her eyes as she left school. No one tried to stop her. She was not surprised.

The first place she could think to go was the McDonald's on Market Street where her cousin made McFlurries. She ate one, Reese's, while she scrolled through her phone. She saw one of those cool, short videos on her Facebook pop up.

A woman with a red blazer and too red lipstick stood in the woods. She gestured over her shoulder and the camera cut to a cave. The yellow type below read:

"Tectonic shift produces Brewer's Yawn in Deschutes Forest. Way to go, Earth!"

Marisol thought while she demolished the remains of the chalky ice cream. It was time for her to shake things up, any ways. She wanted to know if she could.

"Gracias, Alandra," Marisol said as she stood up to leave.

"De nada, Marisol," her cousin called, priming another sundae.

Marisol hopped on the bus to say a good-bye she would regret not making. She didn't *want* to go, any ways, but she had, after all, reached her limit. The breaking apart is just as important as the sticking around.

Ripping off a band-aid is the easiest allegory for how it all goes. But it often doesn't feel that way. It's more like the band-aid gets inched back, adhesive ripping and ripping as long as it takes, until it is good and ready. It's worse that way. But it's often more meaningful.

She had thought about this for a long time. It had been months coming. Since the election it had gotten so dense in Marisol's world—so *hard*. It was like some bully took a flash light and shoved it on top of her house, breaking some of the shingles.

Chapter 2

Oakland's Youth Center was full of brightness and light. A dozen different kind of vegetables thrived in the planter style barrels. Marisol took the AC Transit over to her usual after school haunt.

"Mary-soul!" a smoker's rasp called out.

A thin drawing of a man stepped out the front door and onto the black top. His hair cut was practical and it offset his gaunt eyes. He smiled like a million bucks, which *also* offset his sunken eyes. A few rambling kids skipped behind him in the part-open door.

"Hey Bob," Marisol said. "I can't stay today."

"That so?" Bob scratched his head. "That's a shame now, idn't it, Mary-soul? Your brothers and cousins will be lookin' for you."

She asked to come in and he led her to the back of the center. There were only a few kids running around, rather than the usual dozens, since school hadn't let out yet. Marisol had taken scheduling into her own hands. They sat at a small white table in the back, where there was a see-saw and a four square court painted on the black top.

"I wanted to ask you to tell my brothers and cousins not to worry about me," Marisol said.

Bob scratched his head even more than usual.

"Why would they worry about you?" he asked.

"I can't tell you that," Marisol said.

"Alright, Mary-soul," he said, raising his hands like she held some kind of weapon. "Alright. I'll tell 'em. Tomas will be the most worried of course."

Marisol winced. She had been thinking about her youngest sibling all day. But she knew they would understand. And she wouldn't be gone long.

"Just tell them, please," she said again.

"I will," he said. "You take care of yourself. If I could keep each of you kids that goes off the rails at this age safe, I would. But I know you've got to do what you've got to do."

Marisol nodded quickly. Bob may have been one of the few adults in her life who understood where she was coming from.

The bus station was only a half-mile away from the youth center. Bolt Bus was swankier than she imagined, but not by a lot. It was cheaper than a Greyhound the whole way, but she did have to transfer in Portland.

"So, sweetie, you'll get off at PDX and head on the 39R over to Bend, okay?" a friendly-seeming man told her at the station.

"Got it," Marisol said.

"That's in about 15 hours, okay?"

"Got it."

"Great, good," the man punched on his keyboard. "Okay! Well good luck, pu'nkin!"

Marisol said nothing and sat outside for her bus. She wasn't in the mood to make men feel better about themselves today.

She took out a notebook and wrote a simple message explaining that she was out to find esperanza. Regrettably the only person that she could leave it with was the friendly-seeming man, but he said that *if* anyone came looking for her, he would give it to them.

"I'm not trying to hurt anyone," Marisol said. "I just need time to do this."

"I'm sure they'll understand," the man smiled.

Marisol didn't want her family to worry. She thought about her brothers. Her poor madre. Her poor padre. But she thought about herself and she knew she had to love herself beyond all of the rest. And that the only way to love them best was to take care of herself first.

The bus was smelly like a middle school locker room. The seats were almost all full, but she found one a few rows back right next to a huge woman. She was enormous—her huge hair was curly and free, and her huge smile was inviting Marisol to join her on the rickety bus seats.

"Thank you," Marisol said softly.

"You don't have to thank me," the woman smiled. Even though it was nighttime she didn't wear a coat or anything. "My spirit shined, like a goddess, and you knew it was okay to sit here."

Marisol didn't say anything.

"That was supposed to make you laugh," the woman winked.

Marisol snorted a laugh.

"Where are you going?"

"I read about a cave in Oregon called Brewer's Yawn," Marisol said. "I thought I would go see it."

"Yeah?"

"Yeah," Marisol said. Her confidence was rising. "Just to see it. And to get away from all the hatred where I live."

"Oh," the woman pulled something out of her purse. "How about this?"

It was a muñeca, a tiny plastic doll that looked sort of like Lana del Rey.

"It's really nice," Marisol said. "What about it?"

"I just thought you'd like it," the woman said. "It's always been a wonderful thing for me in confusing times. My o-bachan gave it to me."

Marisol took the doll. It was so simple, just a woman in a red dress. She turned it over, smiled at the woman, then put it in her backpack. She buttoned her fleece all the way up to her chin as the bus got rolling. Someone had their window cracked and the cold air nipped at Marisol's legs—her jeans had holes in the knees.

"I think you're going to be a-okay, girl," the woman said to Marisol. She was leaning her head against the window, her eyes shut.

"Gracias," Marisol said under her breath. "Yo pienso la misma cosa."

Marisol only had one dream once she got to sleep. In it she had found the mouth of the cave and was walking up to its darkness. Some great noises were churning inside the cave, but Marisol ignored them and walked further toward the Yawn. From inside the darkness, as she was about to enter, some brilliant sheen struck her eyes, like a prism of white light.

The light overtook all of her dream, and she woke up.

Chapter 3

DANTE McCORMICK WAS TIRED of that scene. The whole "let's go out" every night thing. It was getting old to pull friends out of an Uber and tuck them into bed, making sure to leave a big steel pot just below their head.

He was a shorter guy, always had been, and he was the one who got the weird looks when they would hit a party. It was usually just him and his friend Michael, the tall and Superman-looking one. Dante gave off a Black and Chicano Wolverine thing. They'd find another kid to run with before they went out, but it was always the two of them at least.

The girls weren't impressed with Dante, but mostly because he never really talked at parties. Everyone was dressed like it was something to celebrate, but sitting in some stranger's living room getting high wasn't a holiday for Dante. It was just a Friday night, or a Tuesday night. And he didn't get high anymore. So he just sat.

"Come on, man," Michael would say. "Just take a hit."

"I'm fine, dude," Dante would reply. "Let's just go soon, okay?"

Michael would shrug and offer to someone else, and the night would go on like that. He didn't like lying to his family very much, so when he did stop, he really felt good.

Dante's last party was about six months ago. That was the last time he had been to that big white house in the South End. Things hadn't gotten *much* better since then, but he was home more. That helped out, or so it seemed.

"You going to school?"

His mom's voice sailed into his ears in ways his phone's alarm never could. Waking up to the *brrt* of a phone wasn't great. He just slept a lot these days.

"No," he mumbled.

She was standing by his door, her eyes peering through the crack into her son's room. It was like seeing a ghost trying to fumble out of a cemetery.

"Could you pick up the dog poop?" his mom asked.

Dante's eyes slouched open. He rose his head a quarter-inch from the pillow and eyed his mom through that same crack in the door. Their eyes met in a most-chalant way.

"Yes."

The shovel was a yellow and black thing that Dante could never get to work just right. He knew that shovels don't really "work right" for anyone, but it just seemed like whenever he tried to use this type of thing he was just horrible at it. It was that way ever since June 27, 2017.

When Martha McCormick left the world it was the most painful day of Dante's life. It was the type of internal shift that signals a huge change. An irreversible type of change.

They had so many plans together, so many little smiles. She knew so much joy and Dante knew that she knew that joy. One time when they were kids, he was ten and she was eight, they played one game of Yahtzee for seven hours. Or it felt that way, and that's what matters.

It had been a stupid party like any other stupid party—stupid. Dante was no newbie, he'd been going to parties before it was cool to go to Tacoma parties, but Martha was just starting. She was only fifteen years old.

Blake Fauntleroy was 19-years-old, and had just graduated high school. He hung out too long like flies around a bowl of fruit. Why hadn't he gone anywhere yet? It didn't matter, since Martha had been dating him since they were both in high school. He was her first everything, and if she had made it to adulthood, that might not have mattered. But, at fifteen, it mattered a lot.

The lights were a thousand different colors. Every scene that night was painted in that glory. Girls wore crazy clothes, boys wore crazy clothes, everyone and their brother was wearing crazy clothes. It was a trap kind of party, not an acoustic guitar kind of party.

Dante sat at a couch in the front room of the big white house. If one could call it a room—it had one wall exposed to the front yard, tattered tapestry dancing as a theoretical door and shelter. Smoke poured out from below and into the streets outside.

He had been playing Cards Against Humanity, a ridiculous drink in his hand, when he noticed that Martha said she would be there hours ago.

"Have you seen Martha?" Dante asked Blake.

Blake's breath smelt like flat beer and Oreos. His yellow teeth hid behind the flashiest grills on any 19-year-old in Washington.

"Naw man," he croaked. "Why, wherezsheat?"

"She said she was with you tonight. When did you last see her?"

He still remembered the glaze that spread over Blake's eyes in that moment. It was the last few hours meeting the possible next few years. Blake was stupid, but he had heard what happened to guys like him. Guys who refused to act their age.

Dante catapulted the family Doberman's poop into the garbage bin. Acting tough at school was lame; it was better to stay at home or just go somewhere else. Going to school *was* lame, but this was plain crappy.

The funeral had been a sickening blow. And rushed. Just as the flower was blooming, it had wilted in just one night. His face was painted in tears. It didn't seem to matter what he did, he just couldn't get the paint off.

Chapter 4

FERN HILL WAS A quiet spot to live. It beat the South End—Dante never went to the South End anymore. He had liked the time they had an apartment along the water, but that was only because Anton, his dad, had such a high-paying job with the city for a while. That was then, this is now kind of stuff.

It's only fun to walk into a walk-in freezer in the summer. Like when it's full of gelato, still setting. Dante would tell his friends to come through during his shift, and the few times they did he made sure to have the hook up. Hazelnut, coconut, and mango sorbet; Sirena Gelato always had the best ingredients.

"Are you going to come to school next week?" one of his not very good friends asked him.

"Eh, this beats going to school most of the time for me. I'm still figuring it out," Dante said.

"Alright," Michael said, licking "Chocolate Chocolate" off of a spoon. "But make sure to come through for the final. I know this job is *chill* and all."

"Yeah, we'll see," Dante said. "Easy on the puns. You'll melt the gelato with that fire."

Once they left he turned back to his freezer-mixer. He was a certified "Vat Technician," as one has to be to make gelato legally. It's all because of some Odwalla lawsuit that had to do with pasteurizing. The lawyer who won the case lives on Bainbridge Island—go figure.

It was a regular Tuesday. Nothing monumental. Not going to Lincoln High School wasn't *that* monumental. Though his parents disagreed.

He finished whipping out another batch of the gelato base—sort of the chicken stock of the ice cream world—and got into his Cutlass Sierra. The few texts from the few girls he was talking to were uninteresting. Most things were.

"Back," Dante said as he dropped his backpack on the floor. It didn't thud when it hit the ground.

"At 1 p.m.?" he heard his mom ask from the living room. Dante walked into the front room to see his mom splayed on the couch. Netflix rambled from her laptop, but her eyes were laser-focused on him.

"I finished my shift," Dante said. "Roger's cool with me taking off as soon as the second batch is freezing."

"I didn't ask if Roger was cool with it," she said. "I don't *care* if Roger is cool with it. I care that you are skipping school. A lot."

"Belinda, Belinda, Belinda," Dante said. "It's allll good. Okay?"

"Not okay," she stood. "Not okay."

Dante picked up his bag and made for the stairs. He didn't listen to whatever his mom was saying, something about when his dad came home. This house didn't feel like a home to *him*, so he didn't know what she was talking about.

In his room he lay on his bed and looked at her pictures on Facebook. The ones that hadn't been removed yet. Mostly photos that were through his own profile, or a profile of one of her friends. Photos of Martha.

He spent most afternoons this way. It was like a cloud hung over his life: work, sometimes school, sitting in his room obsessing and dealing with his parents who were constantly unhappy with the choices of his life. It felt like nothing could change.

His mom's voice carried up the stairs. Then Dante heard the door open, close. A roar came from his dad. Dante knew the drill.

His feet scudded down the stairs and into the lion's den.

"Hey Dad," Dante said.

At the table his dad stood up. He was still in his tie and buttoned shirt, still ready for business. They locked eyes.

"Why aren't you going to school? Who gives a shit about making gelato? You don't need money, Dante," his father said, his voice as collected as he could muster.

"I care about school less than I care about gelato, apparently," Dante said.

"Don't be a smart ass," his dad said.

"Anton, he's grieving," Belinda said.

"But it's not okay," Anton said.

"It's not okay, Dante," Belinda said. "He's right about that."

"Is this Good Will Hunting? I don't think what happened to her is my fault. Can we just eat?"

The three hushed themselves in the awkwardness that they had created. They ate baked potatoes and ribs, with a side of fruit salad. The potatoes steamed once cracked open.

"It's not your fault, Dante," Belinda whispered. "She made her choices."

"She didn't know any better! And now I can make choices that help all of us! I can make things better!" Dante exploded.

"The best choice you can make is to finish *school*," Anton said, his voice boiling. "That's what Martha would have wanted for you."

"You have no *idea* what she would have wanted. None of us do—we hardly ever saw her. She was always in the South End."

"So that's what you're going to do then? Be a big man and hang out in the South End?"

"No, no. I'm gonna get out of here," Dante said. He pushed his potatoes to one side of the plate and drove his fork through the middle. "I'm headed to Michael's after dinner."

"Alright, Dante, but just know that no one is trying to control you or hurt you or anything. It's all in love," his mother said.

"Yeah whatever," Dante said.

After eating the rest of the admittedly delicious potatoes and diced fruits, he fled upstairs. He packed socks, underwear, shoes, toilet paper, a toothbrush, a notebook, and some pictures of him and Michael, some of him and Martha. He decided he wouldn't need pictures of his mom and dad, even though he loved them. It would just hurt more than he wanted it to.

The Greyhound station was right by I-5, attached to a Chevron. With his duffel bag and in his hoodie, he felt like a target—like anyone in this dominantly White state could take him for some type of thief or thug. The fact that it was night, and that everyone waiting for the bus looked like they could be some type of thief or thug, didn't necessarily make things better. It didn't necessarily make them worse, though.

In a dribble of rain, Dante got on board 38A headed South toward Oregon. He just wanted to feel like he could make change in his life. Like the things he said about doing for Martha could be done. Sitting with his head resting against the window, he wasn't so sure they could.

But he was tired of resting his head against the desk, the few times he went to school anymore. He was tired of moving batches of ice cream to and from a big Frankenstein looking machine in the corner of a tiny processing plant. And he was tired of feeling so powerless.

The thoughts in his head were rampaging, like dogs barking, and it felt good to leave them at the bus stop.

Chapter 5

His dad's Prius purred gently outside as Jerrold got ready for school. It wasn't that cold, but his dad always said that it *was* a Prius after all, and if they wanted it as toasty as possible then gosh darnit it just could be.

He jammed his feet into his Converse and bolted toward the door. A banana and packet of peanut butter was in his left hand, and his book bag was in the other. Jerrold called it a book bag, but no one else at school bought into his old-timey way of talking.

"Bye, darling," Jerrold's mom called to him. She did a 180 on her medicine ball chair to wish him farewell. "Did you grab your breakfast?"

"Yeah," Jerrold said. "All two pieces of it."

"And you've got your lunch?"

Jerrold stopped at the door and dashed into the kitchen. On the island in the middle, a wonderfully upper class thing, he spied a brown sack lunch with tiny, well-portioned tupperwares inside. Dry nuts, leafy greens, quinoa: that type of lunch. All went inside his book bag.

"Bye, Mom," Jerrold said. He ran into her office to give her a farewell hug.

"Remember to study hard, remember to tell Mr. Donovan that you have a lacrosse meet on the day of the spelling bee, and remember to finish your application to run for treasurer," she grabbed his face and shot off each word like a machine gun.

"That's next year's election," he rolled his eyes.

"But you need to be ready."

He liked riding to school in his dad's car. The Prius gets a bad rap, but he thought it was a solid rig.

"Okay, buddy," his dad said, checking over his shoulder before the Prius hit the black top. "What are we doing today?"

"Studying hard. Lacrosse meet. Treasurer application," Jerrold repeated.

"And?"

Jerrold froze. He looked at his dad. The bearded progenitor was smiling, but Jerrold didn't trust him.

"I don't know," Jerrold said. "I don't know."

"Picture day packets! Picture day packets."

"Oh," Jerrold said. "Well you could've told an old geezer like me! I forget easy these days!"

They both laughed, but Jerrold felt sad. He could never get them all right. The high school he went to now was a bit further away from where his middle school had been, but that wasn't a problem. All the more chance to ride in the Prius, and for his dad to *drive* the Prius.

"Okay buddy," his dad said. "Have a great day! Remember your tasks, okay?"

Jerrold had a witticism prepared, but instead decided to just smile at his dad. Then he got out of the car and ran into school.

The world went right for Jerrold Hepler. That's what it felt like to everyone else. If you looked at the 14-year-old, you'd see a sandy blonde-haired, blue-eyed 'regular' kid. His whiteness made him the default. The default funny class president. The default decent athlete. The default mover and shaker.

His friends knew him as Jerry Seinfeld. He was always the kid who could get on top of a desk and sing the new Taylor Swift song and always the kid whose test you wanted to cheat off of. Nobody seemed to pull off middle school as well as Jerrold Hepler, and no one was pulling off ninth grade as well, either.

"Dear Jerry," a note in his locker read. "You're the funniest. And the cutest. Text 260–851-8926 and let's meet up."

He looked around and saw nobody, but texted the number.

> Jerrold: *This is Jerry, who is this?*
> 260-851-8926: *Toby Manderson. Do you want to meet up?*
> Jerrold: *Yeah I'll meet up. Where?*
> Toby: *The flag pole. Right after school.*
> Jerrold: *Cool.*

When sixth period came to a close, and that familiar dinging of the bell rang throughout the school, Jerrold collected all of the butterflies in his stomach and went toward the flag pole. He saw Toby, with his dark brown hair that made him look like Edward from Twilight. But he also saw his dad's Prius.

"Hey Jerry," Toby said. "Thanks for coming."

All the kids around them were moving to and from the parking lot like the schools of fish in Finding Nemo. But Jerrold knew they were watching him. And so was his dad.

"Yeah Toby," Jerrold said. "What did you want, any ways?"

"Just to hang out," Toby said, smiling.

"But you're a tenth grader," Jerrold said.

"A tenth grader who knows a cutie when he sees one," Toby said.

"I can't talk about that right now," Jerrold said. "I have to go get my packet for picture day."

He turned around, and a few kids started snickering. Toby looked around, his face stop sign red, and carried himself off toward the buses.

Jerrold feigned being upset that he forgot the packet, since his face was still a little red when he asked Ms. Stazincsky at the front desk for a picture packet. He stuffed it in his back pack, crushing the note from Toby underneath.

"Buddy," his dad said. "How'd the tasks go?"

"Great," Jerrold said. "Knocked 'em all off."

As they drove home Jerrold felt a bee's nest in his stomach. It was whirring and angry, but he couldn't quite make out why he should be upset. For doing everything so well, why was he so confused about this one thing?

It wasn't just that he had a crush on Toby, though. There was an extra layer to why he was embarrassed that kept gnawing at him. *That* thing he just couldn't see.

Jerrold tossed his book bag in the mudroom of their sleepy home. Eugene, Oregon, might be a beautiful place to be, but anyplace that someone isn't allowed to be themselves isn't that beautiful.

Jerrold's mom was in the kitchen listening to NPR's "How I Built This." She was a business owner, and it was *crucial* for her to do her research, she said.

"School," his mom said. "School school school. Did we get those tasks knocked out, Jerry?"

"Yeah, Mom," Jerrold said. "Fun stuff!"

"Oh good sweetie," she smiled as she hugged him. "I'm working on a risotto with eggplant. Don't knock it 'til you've tried it Jerrold, really."

"Alright, Mom," Jerrold said.

He went to his room in the rambler style house. Posters of David Bowie and Spider-Man watched over him as he changed. Before going back to the living room he sat on his bed, exhaling the day. A few tears welled in his eyes before he really started crying.

"Hey dinner in five, Jerrold," his dad called. "We gotta work on that ASB speech right after, okay?"

"Okay, Dad," Jerrold said.

He threw on a tee shirt and went to the dining room. It was cold in his room when he left.

Chapter 6

"Okay sweetie it's time for lacrosse practice."

Nadine called for her son from the front room. He winced when he heard her voice. Jerrold knew his parents meant well but it was becoming a strange performance, him feeling like the bonobo with the banana.

He wasn't even *good* at lacrosse. And he certainly didn't like it. It was just one of the number of things that if he did well, his parents would talk to him for almost an hour. And that was awesome.

"Coming!" Jerrold grabbed his bag for practice. But inside he didn't have any of his sports gear. No mask, or jersey, or cleats. Though he did have his stick, he had crammed the bag full of snack bars, Spider-Man comics, and Goosebumps books.

When his mom left him at the Rec Center, he waited for her tail lights to round the corner before he took off running. He made it almost a mile before he started to walk, arms above his head.

Heading East was the opposite of what all the annoying old White guys had done in the name of Manifest Destiny. So that's where he wanted to start—heading East. Bend seemed like as good a spot as any.

The bus was intimidating. Lots of strangers, and he was by far the youngest passenger. Some of the other passengers seemed to look at him like a piece of cheese. In a time of ride-shares and Couchsurfings, the Greyhound felt alien.

"You sure you're on the right bus, kid?" an old black man asked him. His scraggly beard was as white and gray as his grandfather's, but his eyes were yellowed and browned. Jerrold sat right in front of him with his bag as the only other guest in his row.

"This one heads to Bend, right?"

"I mean that you're not on, like, a *school* bus," he said.

"I'm trying something new," Jerrold thought out loud. "I feel like Mr. Ed sometimes. Like I'm an exciting thing to look at, and that I do a good job all things considered, but that I'm just a trained animal."

"I understand," the man reclined, a worry gone from him. "So you're on some type of self-discovery thing?"

"I guess so," Jerrold said. "I've always taken myself for a real conquistador."

"What?"

"Bad joke," Jerrold said. "Sorry."

"It's fine, lil' buddy," the man put a tired hand on Jerrold's shoulder. "Try and relax. It's already 7:30, you're probably whupped."

"Yeah, I guess so."

"It's a long bus ride. So try and get some sleep."

"How long?"

"Oh, eight hours or so?"

"Jeeze," Jerrold said.

He took out a chunk of the clothes he had packed and balled them into a headrest. Between his cheek and the rain-wet window it worked to cushion some of the craziness of what he felt. He had his cell phone, so he wasn't *so* worried, but he had it on airplane mode for a reason.

Just for a second, though, he flipped on reception. Jerrold didn't fancy Instagram or Twitter—they seemed toxic. But he checked his text messages. Twelve texts from his parents, but he expected that and a few missed call. But he had one more in his inbox. This one from Toby.

Toby: Hey

The bus chugged to life. As they pulled out of the lot and rattled toward Highway 126, Jerrold smiled, excited by change. It was scary, but he had to smile.

Jerrold: Hey yourself. You're not going to see me for a while at school but don't say anything.

Almost no time passes before the screen flashes a new banner.

Toby: Why? I'll miss seeing your shiny self walking by Ms. Donovan's room.

Jerrold: Because I'm done with that stuff for a while. I need to take some time to be alone. Or away from that stuff anyways.

Toby: What stuff?

Jerrold: School stuff, lots of stuff stuff. My parents really exhaust me.

Toby: Oh I'm sorry. If you want to talk I'm here.

Jerrold didn't know what to say—he hadn't heard that from anyone in what felt like a very long time. He had dropped his phone in his lap, and as he picked it up to switch it to airplane mode again, he got one last text:

Toby: <3

Jerrold's face went red and he switched his phone to airplane mode, then off. He crammed it in his sports bag.

Sleeping felt like its own act of resistance—like he was supposed to be working hard even now. There was always an essay to write, or some homework to crunch through. But not now.

He just slept. And his dreams were swirls of fantasy and possibility.

Chapter 7

IT WAS AN OVERNIGHT bus trip. It didn't feel too jarring when Dante stepped off around five a.m. He had let his anxiety go, and wasn't too invested in his depression right now, either. Five a.m. works just as well as five p.m., he figured.

The bus stop had a Perkin's just across the parking lot. After collecting his bag, he walked himself toward the breakfast spot. It was just opening, and he was led to a table near the case of pies and muffins. Each one perfect.

"Could I please have a chocolate cream cheese muffin?" he asked the server.

"Certainly," she smiled.

Dante grabbed the base of the muffin to root it to the plate. With his other hand he took his knife and began to saw at the base of the muffin. He separated half of its base, then flipped it on top. He'd learned this trick on YouTube—a muffin sandwich.

It tasted like Sunday church with Martha. As kids the two of them would slog through the service, doodling on the check-in cards like mad, then rush to the coffee and pastries. Standing there, hovering to make sure the best treats were theirs, was the best part about Sundays.

It was a Wednesday now. He sighed.

Jerrold was just getting off of his bus not too far from Dante at all. The friendly fellow who sat behind him was helping Jerrold get his bag off the bus. The bright-eyed but very sleepy 14-year-old saw the same friendly lights at Perkins that had lured Dante, so he lugged his gear that way, too.

The server sat Jerrold at a booth just in front of Dante's. He was facing the muffin-eating stranger, and smiling.

"What?" Dante asked.

"Oh," Jerrold caught himself and looked down. "I'm so tired. I just was looking into space."

"That's okay," Dante said. "I'm bushed, too."

Jerrold ordered an orange juice and one of those cartoonishly over-sized chocolate chip cookies. They came in short order.

"Are you alone?" Jerrold asked.

Dante didn't answer. He stopped eating, and set his muffin down, then looked out the window. The sun was just starting to come out.

"I think so," Dante said. "You?"

"Yeah," Jerrold said. "Well, my parents wouldn't think so. But they're not making it easy on me. It's confusing. I think they've texted me a bunch of times."

"Mine too," Dante said. "I just put my phone on airplane mode. It's not like I *want* to talk to them."

"Wait," Jerrold said. "Did you leave home, too?"

"Um, yeah," Dante said. He stuffed the rest of his muffin in his mouth. "Didn't you?"

"Yeah," Jerrold said. "It's just what I had to do."

"Right," Dante said. "I had to get out of there. I brought some good reading material, though."

"Yeah?" Dante asked.

Jerrold picked up his plate and went to sit by Dante. This confused Dante a bit, but he was alright with the new company. Jerrold pulled out Spider-Man comics, the Miles Morales stuff, and showed it to Dante.

"I'm Dante," he said after they had been reading a while.

"I'm Jerrold! The Jer-bear. Jerroldus Maximus."

"Ha, okay, Jerrold," Dante said.

Then the door jingled again. There was still almost no one in the res-taurant: the staff and two older White men in trucking caps sipping not-good coffee in the corner. But in walked one more customer.

Marisol had her backpack on one shoulder, and an Arco gas station bag from across the street. She looked exhausted.

Dante and Jerrold watched her as she was given the table that Jerrold had just been seated at. She sat in front of their booth, so Dante could look right at her. Jerrold sipped his orange juice, stuffing his comics in his bag.

After Marisol ordered a coffee, which impressed Dante and Jerrold deeply, Jerrold spun around.

"Are you alone, too?"

Marisol was stunned. The sleepy eyes beneath her glasses went wide. She said nothing.

"Oh, sorry," Jerrold said. "Dante and I are alone. Well not anymore. But we thought you might be alone, too. We could all be alone together!"

Marisol stared at Jerrold. Dante and Jerrold stared at Marisol. In the silence the server brought Marisol's coffee. The heat painted her glasses the same way a shower paints the mirror.

"Uh," Marisol began. "I'm *not* alone. I have friends outside."

"Oh, okay," Jerrold said.

"Wait, uh, that was just to make sure you weren't doing anything creepy," Marisol said. "I'm alone. I just left Oakland yesterday."

"Oakland as in *California* Oakland?!" Dante asked. "Why'd you come all the way here?!"

"I was tired of feeling so useless," she said quietly. "I couldn't hold on anymore."

"Hey," Jerrold said.

Marisol looked up at her restaurant mates. They were smiling tiny and optimistic smiles.

"Come sit with us!"

Marisol took her coffee and, tentatively, joined her fellow overnight vagabonds. They talked about each other's food, about where they were from, how they had *any* money, and about why they came to Bend, Oregon. A frozenness began to thaw.

"I just bought a ticket that worked with when I was supposed to be at lacrosse practice," Jerrold said. "It was totally random."

"You think so? I just found a ticket for when my parents thought I'd be at a friend's place. Same kind of thing."

"Oh," Marisol laughed, then steadied herself. "That wasn't my situation at all. Have you heard of Brewer's Yawn?"

She told them about the video she'd seen. About some kind of geological happening in the Deschutes Forest. They got on Google.

"'Brewer's Yawn,'" she read aloud from a news article. "'Has been determined to be of little geological significance. A seismographic shift in microtectonics has caused a mound of earth about fifteen feet high to rise from the ground.' That was only yesterday."

"You came here for *that?*" Dante asked.

"It seemed important," she said. "Or at least worth seeing. I had never been so unsure about what to do, and it seemed like a sure thing."

"You got me there," Dante said. "I'd be into seeing that."

"Me too!" Jerrold said. "It's not like I have anything else planned for the next, ya know, rest of my life."

The three of them laughed like people who are just meeting each other do—hopeful and nervous.

"You two could come, if you wanted," Marisol said. "I'm going to see it today."

"Wow, I'd love to!" Jerrold said. "What do you think, Dante?"

"I'm about it," Dante said. "I really don't care, Jerrold. It's not Tacoma, so that's pretty good."

"Okay," Marisol said. "I guess we should get going."

She stood up to pay. Dante and Jerrold looked at her, their mouths full of Perkin's.

"I thought you were coming?"

They scrambled to pick up their bags, and followed their new leader to the front counter. Marisol lay out dollars like a bank teller, with intention and precision. As she did, it dawned on Jerrold and Dante that she was the *jefe*. They both learned something right then and there about the Oakland native with the multi-colored fleece.

Chapter 8

BEND HAD SO FEW people. In comparison to Tacoma and Oakland, it was a ghost town. For Jerrold, Bend was still pretty exciting, but for the city goers it was remarkable how sleepy it seemed. The three seemed to forget that on a Wednesday morning most of this city would be working or in school. These particular institutions were not of immediate relevancy to them anymore.

Marisol had helped them find a bus that would ramble into the center of town. They had looked at their collective money and decided it was too precious to waste. Which was another way of saying they had decided they had almost none, and would need to be careful.

It was, after all, only the first morning of their big trip. The trip where they'd finally make a difference.

The municipal bus system was no train, but it took them in decent time to the center of town. The huge trees that Marisol had seen become more and more frequent during her ride north were just common place here. Even Dante, who was surrounded by water and lots of beautiful plants, was floored.

Jerrold thought that Bend was prettier than Eugene, but not by a lot. He had always loved how all of Oregon had a scenic way to itself, a quiet niceness that pervaded the whole state.

Their bus driver didn't mind the fact that three kids were riding alone. She actually seemed to be proud of them. Dante kept worrying that someone would sell them out, and Marisol had agreed when he had said as much. But she told them that they had to keep going. They had all agreed then.

Their bus dropped them off of Highway 97 at a semi-busy intersection. They took in their surroundings—sort of suburban, sort of urban, lots of coniferous trees.

"Feels familiar," Jerrold said.

"Not to me," Dante said.

"Me neither," Marisol said.

The Latina looked over her left shoulder and saw a tiny store. It had a dangling sign that read "Art You Glad We Don't Sell Orange?" She walked up to the window.

Inside she saw paint brushes and canvases and marionette models of all sizes and kinds. Her face lit up when she saw a dirty kiln at the back of the store.

Dante and Jerrold watched her go in, then followed. The whole store was full of fun things like portraits of pugs and little wire chickens made of scrap metal. Marisol was drawn to the pottery, and without even asking, she began to mold a brick of clay that she found. Dante flipped through a sketch book, and Jerrold helped himself to a dish of free Dove chocolates at the counter.

Someone cleared their throat right behind her. A freckled woman in a green smock looked down at Marisol. Her hair looked like a sheep that had just been electrocuted.

"Uh, I'm sorry," Marisol started.

"You haven't even put on a smock," the woman said. "Here."

She lifted the green smock that she was wearing up and over her frizzy orange hair and gave it to Marisol. It was big on her, but she said gracias.

"It's no problem," the woman smiled. "I'm glad someone came in here at all. I've only been in business a few weeks and it's hard to get people to try it out!"

"You *own* this place?" Marisol asked.

"Yeah," she said. "I was working in graphic marketing for like ten years, stowing money away in a nest egg. I had a husband who was going to open up shop with me, but he sucked."

"He sucked?"

"It's complicated. But he was a bozo. He didn't appreciate the power of art like I did. Any ways, have fun back here, kid. Let me know if you need anything."

The woman walked back to her station at the front counter. Marisol was speechless. She turned into her brick of clay and began to knead, wetting her hands as she had to, and she began to create.

Eventually Dante and Jerrold came back to find her. Jerrold raised an eyebrow when he saw her so engrossed.

"You ready to go, Marisol? It's awesome here but we should see more of the town," Jerrold said.

"Plus I thought you wanted to see this Brewer's Yawn deal?"

Marisol finished her work and set it down. It was a sunflower, replete with stems and some well-pressed pedals. She grinned. The three walked to the front of the store, and as they passed the owner Marisol turned and said:

"You inspire me, so I made a flower to inspire you," Marisol said.

"Thank you. That means a lot."

The three took off down the street, chatting about how cool it is to just *make* things.

It was such a sleepy day in the town, they almost couldn't find anything to do. But somehow they kept rambling, peeking inside stores where they couldn't afford anything. Dante and Jerrold took turns jumping over fire hydrants to see who could get the highest. Dante won when Jerrold said fire hydrants were so far below his IQ level it was just showing off to jump over them, any ways.

After the punny art store and trundling around, Dante spied a sports store. Something like a Big 5 but with less variety and a higher price point.

"You want to go in there, Jerry? I bet they could talk lacrosse with you."

"Eh," Jerrold said. "I'm fine. Sports are sort of overrated. But I *am* hungry. How about you two?"

"Definitely," Dante said.

"I see a Safeway, let's pick up some food," Marisol said.

They strolled through aisles of kombucha and too-expensive produce. Each allowed themselves $5 for lunch. Jerrold got peppers and a big tub of hummus, Dante got beef jerky and a bag of Fritos, and Marisol picked up a sourdough sandwich with ham and cheese.

With their spoils in hand they strolled down a winding, semi-industrial road until it led them to the water. A sign read "Dohema River," and they set themselves down there.

"Okay," Marisol said. "I want to trust you guys."

Dante tore at his jerky and Jerrold scooped hummus, their eyes on Marisol as they waited for what she might say next.

"It's just a hard time to go around trusting people you don't really know," she said.

The three sat in silence. The sounds of their lunching got to a point that Dante's anxiety couldn't handle much longer.

"Well," Dante scratched his head. "I'm eighteen and I don't think I'm going to finish high school."

"Really?" Marisol asked. "I'm sixteen. Why wouldn't you finish school?"

"My high school sucks?" Dante said.

"Oh," Marisol said.

"No, sorry," Dante said. He waited a while. "My sister died."

Jerrold and Marisol put their food down and waited. When nothing else happened, Jerrold said:

"I'm sorry, Dante."

Marisol nodded, her eyes swollen.

"Times are weird in Tacoma," he said. "It's going through all this change, with big companies moving all around, but there are still so many kids doing stupid stuff. And Martha was into that stuff. I was too for a little bit."

"Going to school *would* suck after that," Jerrold said.

"I just picked up a job making gelato. My parents gave me some leeway for a while, trying to be understanding and all, but it's getting to them, too."

"I don't think *anything* gets to my parents," Jerrold said. "It's like they don't see me at all."

"What do you mean?" Marisol asked.

"It's nothing like losing a sister, but I feel so. . .alone, when I'm around them. They're both so intense. Always trying to get my grades up, trying to get me to audition for a new play, always something. They don't give me a minute to be myself. It's just 'son do this' and 'son do that' and I don't even KNOW if I'm their son, I just feel-"

"It's okay, Jerry! Slow down," Dante said. It flashed in his mind that he was speaking to his anxious self almost as much as Jerrold, the moments when the barking dogs in his head wouldn't be quiet.

"Ah," Jerrold sat back and scooped another bit of hummus. "It's just too much. I couldn't stay anymore."

Marisol looked at the water. She saw it move backwards and forwards seemingly at the same time. Small fish darted around below the surface.

"I feel like I can never go home," Marisol said. "There's so much hate. No quiero vivir en ese vida. My dad doesn't seem to care that he hates people, and my mom doesn't seem to care that he hates people, and all the kids at school don't seem to care that they hate an *entire* people. My people."

Dante and Jerrold looked out at the water, too. Their tee shirts caught the summer sun on their arms, but they still wore goose pimples.

"It's such a hard world," Marisol said. "And I'm only sixteen. It makes me think that it only gets *worse*. I don't want to think that way."

"I get that. It's why I took off," Dante said.

"Me too," Jerrold nodded.

Marisol ate the rest of her sandwich in one bite.

"I guess I trust all that," she smiled. "You both remind me of a man I know back in Oakland. He's pretty understanding. But he never says my name right."

"That's messed up," Dante said. "I can't believe it when White people call me 'dan-tee.' I mean, who hasn't heard the name Dante at this point?"

The three of them talked about nothing for a long time, walking around the water and throwing things just for the sake of throwing things. Jerrold performed for them a monologue he had to memorize for his audition to Peter Pan. Dante played them his favorite music off of Spotfiy, most recently some Kanye West, on his phone—the saved stuff, so he didn't leave airplane mode. Marisol regaled the other two with a long story about how her family came to be American citizens rather than settlers becoming Mexicans. The fish in the river splashed about.

"I'm actually," Dante yawned. "Really tired."

"Me too," Jerrold said. "Could we just nap for a little while?"

"That works for me," Marisol said. "I'm not worried."

Jerrold took out a small pillow he had stuffed inside his bag. Each of the other two crafted a makeshift pillow, Marisol from her backpack and Dante from some clothes stuffed inside a sweater. Underneath some generous trees, they slept for three few hours. It was as restful as though they'd been at home, especially since none of the three really felt a strong desire to go home at all.

After a few hours they picked themselves up and started to walk again. They saw signs for "Old Bend" and took themselves through more semi-industrial byways. A few cars slowed down to stare at the three, or to swerve unnecessarily out of their lane, but they were left alone as they relocated.

Old Bend had a friendly style. There were lots of cafes and bars, and each had clever sandwich chalkboard messages out front to draw in potential eaters and drinkers.

A favorite of Marisol's: "My superpower is making wine disappear. What's yours?"

They walked all the way down the main drag, and when that ended, they walked all the way down each off shoot street. It seemed like they could just go on forever, not having anything really matter, and that they'd be fine just doing that.

But there was an uneasiness—a tension. It was there between them, a knowledge that no matter what, they would have to deal with why they left.

They found a camping goods store and decided to make some investments. Marisol purchased a hammock, as did Dante, and all three picked up flash lights. They hit the streets again, ready for their spelunking adventures.

After another dead end, they turned around and hit the intersection of that main drag again. An apartment building lay on their left, and just to their right was an eccentric, vine-laden café. A big painted sign above the door read "The Ore-gone-ian"

"You seem lost," a voice called out.

The three flipped around. Emerging from behind the café was a tall white man with hair only on the sides of his gumdrop shaped head. He moved forward with a skippy step.

They said nothing. It was hard to trust anyone anymore. But slowly, like children in a thick fog, they began to walk toward the entrance to the café.

Chapter 9

THE THREE STARED AT the balding man. He had the same walrus mustache many old men do, and he even had the huge gut, too, but his eyes were opals. He had kaleidoscopic eyes like prisms that reflected each bit of sun that they caught in little shards of pink and silver.

"Please," he called them with his hand, flapping like a seal. "Come inside."

"We don't know you," Dante said.

"Well let's fix that up! I'm Howard Rightmore. I run this establishment."

"Hard to argue with that," Jerrold smiled.

"How can we trust him?" Dante whispered to Marisol. "We just barely started trusting each other."

"We can't," Marisol said, her eyes never leaving Howard. "But let's see what he has to offer."

The inside of The Ore-gone-ian was homey. It felt like stepping into an antique shop placed inside a grandmother's home. There were leather couches with brightly designed tables in between them. Magazines with bikers and hikers lay around the café, and one wall had a "Place Your Pin, Pinhead!" board with a huge map with lots of multicolored tiny dots sticking out.

Jerrold took a pin from a paper cup and sprouted his parent's house. In the view of the whole world, he'd only gone an inch or so.

"Let's sit on the patio," Howard said. He stooped over and, like a cartoon, supported himself with one hand on his waist as he slugged along with a cane in the other.

"Why would you want to help us?" Marisol asked.

"Look at the name! The Ore-gone-ian is for lost fish, like you!"

"Fish? What the hell?" Dante said.

"You all were going upstream, living your lives, like any of us can, until something happened. And you said, 'I've got to get out of this fish-race and onto some dry land.' You're exploring! Finding yourselves."

"The only thing that's *fishy* around here," Jerrold started.

"Not now, Jerrold. And thank you, but we just happened to meet at a bus stop. We're all going to see the cave. For fun."

"Is that what you still think?"

Howard sat up, the sun glazing his glasses and making it near impossible to see his eyes.

"There's nothing ordinary about you three coming together. This is a drawing."

"Like Pictograms?" Jerrold asked.

"*Not now*, Jerrold. The cave is a drawing?"

"A summoning. There's more to it than meets the eye. It's no tectonic shift. It's certainly not a random geological burp. It's unearthing itself."

"What is?" Dante asked.

Howard stood up and walked inside the café without a word, his off-brand sandals scuffing along the cement. The three just looked at each other for a moment until he returned, carrying a tightly wrapped leather journal.

"My dad was an Oregonian, and his dad and his. It's been a thing for a while. And in allll that time this journal has been around. It's a guide."

"To what? Local hikes and great flights of beer?"

"Good one, Dante," Jerrold said.

"No, there's about a thousand of those. This is a guide to Oregon throughout the years—topographically."

"Like maps and stuff?"

"Physical maps, yes. Interviews with the Native people who lived here all along, and still do."

"Wow," Marisol said. "I wonder what interviews with my Mexican ancestors would have been like."

"We'll go to the library sometime and find out!" Howard said, unwinding the journal and spreading it on the table.

"Really?" Marisol asked.

"Just so," Howard winked. "Take a look at this, fishes."

The three crowded around Howard and looked over his shoulder to see the pages he wanted them to see. A regal drawing of a beautiful Kalapuya

Native man was next to some calligraphic writing. And below both was a rough sketch. It looked like it could be a question mark, or a trombone.

"What is it, Howard?" Jerrold asked.

"My great-grandpappy wrote this entry about a man he met and the sword he showed 'em. It had been just discovered, then, some type of powerful artifact. It stands to reason it wasn't a European that left the tool, and since it isn't a Chinook or Klamath weapon, it makes one think there's something abnormal about the thing.

'The magic of a dreamcatcher and the strength of the Winahl' he wrote. That's what the Kalapuya people call the Columbia River."

"Wow. So it was a tool?" Dante asked.

"A sword," Howard said, beginning to bring the papers together again, stuffing them in the journal to be wrapped up like a mummy. "But the two decided to toss it in a deep well. It was 'all the control we could never be true to use,' they said. Said they couldn't make use of it in their world."

"You think Brewer's Yawn has something to do with *that?*"

"I do, fishies."

"What's the cave going to be like then? If that thing *is* in there?" Jerrold asked.

"Go in. Find out. I can't tell you that."

The three sat at the faded black and green table with their aging host. He sipped on a green tea and smiled, the gaps in his teeth releasing no more secrets.

"Gracias por su hospitalidad," Marisol said. "Let's go, guys."

"Take some peanut butter cookies for the road. Fish gotta' eat."

Howard extended a bulk bag of his delicious treats, tied together with a tiny white bit of wire. Jerrold snatched the treasure from his hand.

"Thanks!"

"See me again sometime, travelers. Don't forget who you are while you're in there."

The three walked down the few steps of The Ore-gone-ian and onto the sidewalk. There was almost no traffic; it seemed like everyone in town must be out at the Yawn.

"We're still going, right?" Jerrold asked. He mumbled the words through a mouth full of cookie.

"We bought all that camping stuff. . ." Dante said. "It'd be dumb to not still at least see it."

"Of course we're going to still see it," Marisol said. "And of course we'll find a way in, too!"

Dante and Jerrold looked stupefied.

"Really?" Dante asked. "You believe that old dude?"

"Even if he's wrong, or just crazy, didn't we all leave home to try and do something important? That seems important to me," Marisol said.

"Damn, alright!" Dante said, smiling.

The cave was first called Brewer's Yawn by a reporter at Huffington Post. Oregonian's love beer—Deschutes Brewing Company is just inside Bend. James Carsbah, the geologist being interviewed at the time, said it could be called that, sure.

MSNBC, CNN, Fox, and the local places had all their teams at the mouth of the cave. But no one had been going inside; it was deemed too small by experts to yield any type of finding. One old White guy on TV was quoted saying that, "While it was a fascinating upheaval of earth, certainly nothing inside would be worth noting as relevant."

"Plus, it's only been about a week since it emerged. Any universities or high schools or whatever need more time to set themselves up for a field day," said their driver, a bearded 20-something with nothing to do.

The three had requested a Lyft, and somehow they'd found one that would take them from Bend to the Deschutes Forest. For $10 each, that sure beat walking.

"Thanks Brian, you're a good guy," Jerrold said as they got their bags out of the back.

"Hey, my mom said I had to pay for my groceries, especially after majoring in Eastern Philosophy with my only plan being going to Taiwan. So don't sweat it."

The three fidgeted and looked at each other.

"Sorry! That was bitter sounding. Believe in yourselves and study whatever you want!"

"Sure, thanks Brian," Dante said as he slung his duffel over his shoulder.

"Lousy FAFSA. . ." Brian muttered as he started up his mom's Datsun. He sped off as the three faced the woods.

"You still have the map, Marisol?"

"Yeah," Marisol pulled out her tourist's guide to the forest. "We're straight ahead. Hear that?"

They stopped and listened. A hum of talking and electrical noises filled the air. Right in front of them, maybe 100 yards. They started toward it. As they snaked through trees and brush, the pristine air, they saw the clearing.

Trees had been knocked over. Boulders and Great Dane-sized rocks lay about like buoys. Huge firs were laying on their sides like an earthquake had slapped the land around. Where their roots had been, rose the maw of the cave. It was like looking at the type of sand castle a kid makes with their feet, where they suck their foot out and make a raised bump of dirt.

Boxy white vans and cop cars were as strewn about as all the plants and rocks. At least forty adults were standing around, milling, as they busied themselves in whatever way they felt they had to busy themselves. Cops sat on logs and talked to each other while news reporters dabbed on foundation and practiced their lines. Grip holders held microphones.

The three stood far enough away to not be noticed. Jerrold began to walk forward when Dante grabbed his collar.

"We're going to have to sneak in, Jerry. They'll have a thousand questions."

Marisol dropped her pack.

"Which means we'll have to wait until dark. Let's set up a camp."

Chapter 10

THEY STRUNG TWO HAMMOCKS between some of the firs that lasted the geological frenzy. Laughing and talking could still be heard from where they had retreated to, but they were well enough away that nobody from that throng would see them.

"Are we going to have a fire? Fires are awesome," Jerrold said, still content munching on his cookies.

"Smoke would be no bueno, Jerrold," Marisol said. "Besides, it's still day. We'll have to go in as soon as everyone leaves. I just thought we could rest for a while first."

"My bus tuckered me the eff out," Dante said as he slid into a hammock. "Those things are *not* comfy."

"Mine either," Jerrold said. "I think my parents would have been unhappy to hear about what damage could have been done to my lumbar."

"I didn't really mind mine," Marisol said. She was feeling a bit meeker again, less sure. While they were in motion she felt confident and decisive—but in these quiet moments, it was harder for her to know if she was making the right choice. What had Howard said about remembering herself?

Their camp was a quiet one until Jerrold spoke up again.

"I'm still hungry," he groaned. "What's the deal with food? It's like we eat, eat, eat and then we just have to eat again. What's up with thaaat?"

Dante and Marisol laughed.

"Is that a Seinfeld?" Dante asked.

"Yeah, I did it for an assembly, once," Jerrold said.

"Pretty good, Jerry. Hey! Jerry! Jerry Seinfeld!"

"Right," Jerrold smiled sheepishly.

"Who's Jerry Seinfeld?" Marisol asked.

"What!? He's hilarious! He's a comedian!" Dante said, jumping out of his hammock.

"Oh, I don't listen to a lot of comedians," Marisol said. "But I do have some more tamales I took from home. You okay with chicken, Jerrold?"

"Yeah, just don't tell my mom, right folks?"

"Alright alright, just give him something so he quits with the standup," Dante winked.

They all had a tamale and chatted in their little clearing. Birds chirped, snakes slithered, and marmots marmotted all around them. Time had flown by when they noticed cars starting to drive out along the road. Headlights flashed in-between trees like Morse code spotlights.

Jerrold creeped toward the cave and saw some vans and cop cars left— but only about a third as many as before. Only some cops sat around, still on their phones or chatting to each other. Almost all the news folk had cleared out, but a couple of intern-level looking members of the press stood by the cave.

"I don't think we could just walk in yet," Jerrold said. "But I don't know if we'll get any better chance than now."

"We gotta get those last couple to take off," Dante said, slapping his fist in his palm.

"Maybe a distraction would work? That always seems to work for TV shows," Marisol said.

"Right. What can we do though?" Dante said.

"I have an idea," Jerrold said. "I brought a lacrosse stick. We could lob a couple of good-sized rocks as far over them as we can. If we make enough noise, I bet they'd check it out."

"Sort of far-fetch'd, man," Dante said.

"It's worth a *lob*, right?"

"To get you to stop making puns? Sure."

The three scoured the area for the best rocks they could find. Then they placed themselves just to the left of the mouth of the cave, still covered by trees and rocks.

Jerrold took Marisol's first.

"Okay, I'm going to put it back in that brush behind them."

He lowered his arms behind him, as Marisol and Dante got out of the way, and catapulted as hard as he could. The rock went straight as an arrow—but way too low. It smashed into the windshield of one of the TV vans.

"I thought you were good at lacrosse?!" Dante asked.

"No, I just play lacrosse! I brought the stick just to practice!"

"What was that?" a cop stood up. The van began to make all kind of a ruckus, flashing its lights like a robot doused in water. The interns and cops all swarmed to the van.

Marisol tugged on Dante and Jerrold's arms as the opportunity presented itself. She darted around the lip of the Yawn and inside, with Dante and Jerrold right behind her. Their bags bumped off of their backs as they half-ran half-crept as far as they could go. In no time at all, it was completely dark.

Chapter 11

MARISOL UNZIPPED HER BAG and fumbled for a headlamp that she bought at the camping store. The little red gadget clicked to life and gave the three a pool of vision.

"Wow," Dante said. "Lemonade from lemons there, Marisol. Way to go."

"Thanks," Marisol said. She buttoned her fleece all the way to her neck. "It's cold in here. Do you two have any light?"

"Howard gave me a lantern," Jerrold said, revealing a Cabella's brand green beacon.

"I just have a headlamp like you," Dante said.

With all three lights put together, the three were able to gain an illuminated look at their surroundings. They had gone far enough in already to not be seen by those milling outside the mouth of the cave. The sides were sloped and rounded, but now that they were further in they saw that, somehow, the cave was flattening out on top and on bottom.

"It doesn't look too promising," Dante said. "But I think there's some more at the back. See that little space?"

He pointed toward a rectangle of room fifteen or twenty yards further in. The three hobbled their way toward it, feeling like Alice as she navigated that first door and its keyhole. The world was shrinking, or they were getting bigger.

"I can squeeze through," Dante said.

"Then we should be alright. Should we go for it, Marisol?"

"Yeah. We came all this way, didn't we? I don't want to go back to Oakland yet."

"I sure don't want to go back to Eugene. My parents are going to put me on a spit, Lord of the Flies style."

"Yeah, I'm not trying to go back to Tacoma anytime soon," Dante smiled. "I gotta use the time I've got."

With that, he oofed and wriggled his way through the crawlspace. It felt like wormcrawling through an iron maiden, but once all three made it through, the cave expanded into a dreamlike world.

They found themselves sitting on a ledge, hardly bigger than all three of their butts next to each other. Below them, a few feet down, was a much bigger shelf that extended to the right and to the left. Each pathway cascaded down like a Hot Wheels racetrack all the way to the base of the huge cave.

"Looks like a maze down there," Dante said. "This is insane."

Marisol shimmied down to the next shelf, her Adidas touching down without a sound. Jerrold and Dante followed, and the three started to walk down to the base of the cave. It was a quiet affair, the majesty of the world around them taking the words from their lips.

A slow drip could be heard from somewhere in the gloom. The darkness around them was growing as the pathways led them away from their only source of meager light—the crawlspace. Each of their sources of light became all the more precious as they went deeper and deeper.

The pathways finally joined with the base of the cave. Behind them was solid rock, and ahead of them was a series of stalagmites and stalactites.

"Look at all the stalagmites," Jerrold whispered.

"That's not what they're called, Jerry," Dante said. "It's stalactite."

"I don't think that's it either," Jerrold said.

"That's not important! Look!" Marisol said. She walked a little further ahead and they could see that through the stalagmites was an opening. It wasn't too wide, just big enough for young people like them to sneak between.

"Why would we go *in* there?" Dante asked. "We could get lost!"

"What if that story Howard told is true?" Marisol said. "Plus, we just got here. I want to explore."

She shimmied into the labyrinth. Jerrold followed right behind, and Dante swallowed his fear and leapt in. As soon as they made it between the pressed spikes, they found themselves on a new path. For the first time in the cave they saw signs of life: patches of moss, tiny beetles that looked like rolly blue mustaches, and bones. Rodent looking bones.

"Gross," Dante said.

"They're kobold bones," Jerrold muttered.

"What?" Dante said.

"They're the bones of a creature called a 'kobold,'" he said. "It's like a rat plus a goblin. Not very smart. Follow bigger creatures."

Marisol and Dante turned their heads toward Jerrold, the combined beams of their headlamps blinding him.

"What are you talking about?" Marisol asked.

"I don't know how I know that," Jerrold said. "But it's true. I see them."

"How? It's so dark," Dante said.

"I don't know, Dante! This stuff is pretty overwhelming!"

"Fair enough," Dante said. "Let's just get through this maze."

They kept plugging ahead. It was simple at first—just walking down the tight path until they hit a wall, then reorienting the only way they could and going forward. But after some time had gone by of walking, reorienting, and walking again, they realized that they must be making some mistake.

"We saw that patch of moss already," Jerrold said. "We're looping in circles."

"Damn," Dante said. "This is starting to stress me out."

"I'm sure we'll figure it out. Let's keep going," Marisol said.

But hours went by. In the middle of the lonely cave it felt like it could have been weeks. They would get on their hands and knees at points and paw at the earth, looking for some Indiana Jones style button or clue. One corner seemed to lead to a new section of the labyrinth, but after a bit more time they'd see that it was the same as before. The hours droned on. Dante was beginning to think his stomach would start eating its way out of his belly when Jerrold spoke.

"We have to look beyond the obvious," Jerrold said.

Again Marisol and Dante turned to look at him, and this time he was sitting down in the middle of the path.

"Giving up, Jerry?"

"No," Jerrold's eyes were closed. "Just looking around."

"How? Your eyes are closed."

"The best insight can come from within," Jerrold spoke softly.

Marisol folded her arms, and Dante just sighed:

"I didn't know we were exploring with Gandhi," he said.

"Wait," Jerrold said. "Dante. Look to your right."

Dante turned to his right and saw the face of a huge stalactite.

"It's rock, Jerry," Dante said.

"Push it. With both hands."

Dante did as he was told, and gave the enormous pylon a hard shove. It didn't budge, so he dug his heels in and pushed as hard as he could. The pillar gave way, and it toppled over. In its place they saw a new path, decorated with more bones. At the end of the path they spied a hole about the size of a man hole cover.

Marisol walked over to Jerrold and helped him stand.

"Jerrold," she put her hand on his shoulder. The cold of the cave made their connection even warmer. "What's going on?"

"I really don't know, gang," Jerrold said. "It's like a part of me woke up in the cave. I'm starting to see things, and feel things, I never have before. And the cave's maps just seem to be a bonus."

Marisol stepped back and stood by Dante. Jerrold shrugged and grabbed a cookie out of his bag. Marisol snickered and Dante just laughed.

"Same old Jerry to me," Dante said. "Let's get going."

They came to the hole and found a ladder that stretched down into a void. There was only blackness. Dante went first, unafraid. Martha's face appeared suddenly in his mind. That's the world Martha went into—a black void, oblivion. I can go into it, too, he thought.

One foot, then another, one hand, then another. Slow and sure he descended. He called to Marisol and Jerrold not to come until he was sure he could make it to the bottom. Little by little he scaled all the way to the base of the very long ladder.

His headlamp revealed almost nothing. The anxiety inside him was swelling, but he remembered why he was here, and who he was. Marisol and Jerrold climbed all the way down soon, and then he felt strong again.

The stalactites and stalagmites were around them, but they could only really make out that it hadn't gotten so much bigger because of what their light *couldn't* show them. It was like they were the only flames in a field of oil.

"Um, let's split up and look for clues?" Jerrold said.

"Can't your third eye power stuff help us at all?"

"I don't know! I haven't really figured it out," he said. "I can tell you there's some weird rocks on that wall."

Jerrold pointed in Marisol's direction.

"That's a good start, why don't we-"

"But there's some weird rocks on pretty much every wall," Jerrold shrugged.

Dante sighed. He walked toward the wall Jerrold indicated, and both Marisol and Jerrold followed. Once the wall came into the range of their head lamps, they could see the rocks Jerrold had seen. Red rocks and purple rocks took turns sprouting out of the ground in a seemingly random fashion. Sometimes there would be three red and a purple—sometimes eight purple might go by uninterrupted.

"Are these dragon eggs or some Harry Potter crap?" Dante asked.

"I think," Marisol said. "I think it's binary."

Now it was Jerrold who was amazed.

"What do you mean?"

"I remember my computer science teacher saying binary is based off of real life," Marisol said. "The patterns that appear in nature. Offs and ons. It's not so complex. Like morse code."

"Marisol," Dante said. "That *is* complex. You're just smart."

"Uh," Marisol said. "Thanks."

She approached the rocks and squatted down. Each rock was a *little* different, but they were basically the same. When she touched the top of one of the red rocks, it glowed an ambient hue for a small moment.

To test her hypothesis, she touched a purple in the same spot. It glowed in the same vibrant light.

Her mind started to crack the code. It was a simple message. She felt like Indiana Jones or some intrepid explorer. But she didn't need anyone's help. She was *doing* it.

She played the rocks like bongos, tapping them as many times as she needed to get the code right. Jerrold and Dante watched like they had front row tickets to a parade.

With Marisol's final tap, an enormous *click* rung in the cave, a great unlocking. Like they were on a huge pendulum, the floor of the cave shifted toward the ladder and away from the rocks. Each rock was sucked back into the earth.

"What did you *do*, Marisol?!" Dante asked.

"I wrote 'We're looking for a sword' in binary," she smiled. "I guess the Yawn knows how to code, too."

Once they stopped moving, the cave looked a bit different. Where the rock-laden wall had been, there was now a gap in the ground, and a tiny earthen bridge extended from their side to the other. The wall had remained, but a hole that looked like a perfectly cut rectangular portal had opened.

The rocks on the other walls had also given way, and another much larger hole opened as well. From far away an odd rumbling came channeling toward them.

While looking back toward the bigger hole, Dante said:

"So I guess we'd better go that way, huh?"

"I think so," Marisol said. "I can go first."

"I think that's a good idea," Jerrold said. "But I have bad news."

The rumbling grew into a drum line. Clawing and cursing rose into a full chorus. Crawling forward from the enormous hole was an army of rat, lizard people. Little angry things that were clipping forward at a ferocious pace, with a ferocious rage on chattering in their teeth.

"Oh my god," Dante said. "Those are the kobolds?"

"Yes," Jerrold said. "Hurry, Marisol. We won't be able to hold them off for very long."

"Hold them off!?" Dante said. "Are you kidding, Jerry?"

"No," he said. "It's the only way."

The little terrors breached the large room and seeped out like water from a spout, messy and all over. They flooded the room and were channeled right at the three of them.

"Hurry up, Marisol!" Dante said.

"Okay, okay," she said. She steadied her breathing. She placed one foot on the bridge and felt it sink under her weight.

A pin drop pierced her heart—how could she have done this? How could she have left her family behind to chase some stupid idea? And now that idea was going to kill her!? How could she have done this?

"Don't forget who you are."

Marisol looked over her shoulder to see Jerrold smiling. Dante had his feet dug into the ground, facing the rat-goblin things. But Jerrold had the warmest look on his face.

"That's what Howard said, right?"

She smiled.

"Right."

Once she put her weight down, the bridge started to quiver. She sprang from that spot to the next, a little further ahead, and from there to the next. In four hops she was over the divide, and the recently formed bridge began to shake even more. It crumbled like dry dirt on the bank of a river, and cracked into little pieces that sank to the bottom of the ravine.

The wave of kobolds hit Dante. They started to climb on his legs and tear at his pants. Little weapons battered against his fists as Dante rained down punches and slaps, trying to keep the things away from him and his friends.

"Ouch," Dante said. "These things suck!"

"Try to keep them back," Jerrold said. "How's it look, Marisol?"

As she peered into the portal of darkness, her headlamp began to flutter on and off. She turned it off and on, off and on, but it was still on the fritz.

"I can't really see," she said. "It looks like another room. Kind of big. A lot of -ites and -mites. I'm going inside."

She stepped inside and was caught immediately in the total bleakness. Like all her confidence had been zapped from her, she stuck her arms out in front of her. The flashes on her headlamp were further apart, and it appeared as though she only existed for a second at a time.

Jerrold sat down on the lip of the ravine, the remnants of the bridge barely noticeable on the lip of the drop. Dante had his arms stretched out with kobolds dangling off of his clothes. The last to scurry into the room were now catching up to their allies. The entire legion of cave-dwellers would be upon them in no time. Jerrold just closed his eyes.

"There is a sword in the darkness," Jerrold called out, his mind seeing what his eyes couldn't. "It's about ten yards in front of you, Marisol. Go on."

Marisol walked ahead, her head lamp still sputtering. She galoshed her way through dingy puddles, and around all the –ites and –mites. Her heart thumped like a chugging engine. The heat of getting her creations made, the love of the world, was stoking like mad inside her.

She stuck out her hand and felt a sharpness against her index finger.

"Oh!" she started.

"Marisol!" Dante called from behind Jerrold, his eyes still toward the oncoming army of kobolds. They were small, duck-sized maybe, but the gnash of their mouths scared him all the same.

"I'm alright! I found it."

"The sword?" Jerrold asked.

"Right," Marisol answered. Her light had given her no advantage, and was totally gone now. The length of the blade was, well, quite long. She could tell by patting along the weapon; it stood upright, and as she neared the pommel she could tell it was stuck. A cast of granite or rock sealed the tool inside an –ite or a –mite.

"Oh no," she said. "It's very stuck."

"Damn," Dante called. The kobolds were overtaking him, climbing on his back and shoulders, and he started to flail at them like a mad man waving away invisible bees. "Try and pull it out!"

"I'm not that strong!"

"Use a different type of strength," Jerrold said. "Just go ahead and grab the hilt."

"What is the hilt? How do you know that, Jerrold?"

"My parents love this kind of thing. Just try it out. We're all still here." Then, after a pause, "and, Marisol, don't forget who you are."

Marisol took a deep breath, tried to center herself and then took the sword's hilt in her hand, or so she presumed since she still couldn't even see her hand in front of her face. It had a grip like clay. She could tell it fit her hand like it had been custom cast just for her.

The sword suddenly began to glow.

It illuminated itself like a beacon in the big cave, a pink, purple, and yellow brilliance. Marisol could see, and Jerrold *just* could, that the sword was a scimitar, curved and proud. It had a large stone inside its flat face, like a large piece of quartz. The hilt was black, and looked like not-yet-cool asphalt. Pliable.

Once she gripped it with both hands, as hard as she could, it felt like three years flew by. The sword beamed brighter and brighter, and Marisol felt like she'd been holding it all of her life. Every time she sat in the bed of the truck. Each time she was told she was too light-skinned or not light-skinned enough. Every time the world had slapped her around, this sword had been there for her. Waiting patiently in the darkness.

The rock encasing the lower part of the blade fell away as Marisol thought of the resilience it gave her. The will to push back. The prison of stone dissolved into pebbles and dust.

"I don't think we can wait any more," Dante yelled. His kicking was getting desperate. Two kobolds had been gnawing at his legs long enough that blood was running down his calf. He would *oof* and *ow* and try to defend his friends, but one or two would get through every now and again, and Jerrold gasped as some began to climb his sweatshirt and pull his hair.

Her eyes flared like suns in the gloom. As the sword rose in her two hands, she swept away the darkness of the cave. From within her poured the light of her home, on the not-so-foggy days, and from her soul.

Each kobold pixelated into memory as the light overtook the cave. Their little weapons, helmets, and the little bites and gashes they gave Dante began to seal back up, like they had never been there in the first place.

As Jerrold looked around, he saw not the daunting network of dark obstacles that they had entered, but a well-lit spelunking kind of place. The type of place his dad would think is the "bees knees." The bridge over the gap was reformed, and it looked much stronger than before.

Dante marveled at his healed wounds, then began to cross the bridge himself. Jerrold joined him. The room they stepped into shared the same warm glow. Everything had changed now that Marisol had retrieved the sword.

"Marisol," Dante said. "How do you feel?"

She was still radiating power. From behind the now falling apart stone where the sword had been held, it looked like wind was gushing across her. Her fleece fluttered around her, long black hair coursed around her shoulders, and her eyes shone like twin lightning bolts.

"Like a goddess," she said. "I know that I can shape the world to be my own."

"I think you did," Jerrold said. "Look around!"

Marisol tried. As she came back to her body, she realized it was just her thoughts behind her eyes that she saw. She was shaping and molding, and she didn't seem to be able to stop.

"I can't," she said. "I mean, I know I can, but I'm pretty overwhelmed."

"Oh," Dante scratched his head. "Can we help?"

"I think I got it," Marisol said. She began to relax her grip on the hilt, even though it felt so right to have her hands right there. The illumination of the quartz began to fade, though the light in the room stayed. Dante looked at his pants—they were completely remade, just like his leg had healed.

The tension dropped. It was like Marisol had come down from a mountain top and had landed underneath it, in this cave. But that cave had a lot of lanterns and warm cocoa.

"Dios mio," Marisol said.

"So that's the sword in the darkness, huh?" Dante asked.

"I saw it the second we came in the cave," Jerrold said.

"Is it the same one that Howard told us about?" Marisol asked. She turned it over in her hands, careful not to grip it too tight.

"It seemed to give you some powers. I bet it is."

"We have to take it with us," Dante said.

"Well, yeah," Marisol said.

Jerrold fidgeted a bit.

"What's wrong, Jerry?" Dante asked. "You can use it, too, right Marisol?"

"Por su puesto," she said, squeaking a bit.

"That's not what I'm worried about. Do you remember what Howard said? About how those two guys buried it? I don't want to lose you two if it *is* a bad idea to take it."

"Aw, Jerry," Dante smiled as he put his arm around Jerrold. "There's no way you're losing us. This sword will bring us closer. We can start fixing the world!"

"Oh, okay! Good," Jerrold said. He leaned his head toward Dante.

"Let's get going," Marisol said. "We can't pretend to know what's going to happen yet."

The three began walking back toward the mouth of the cave. Each was overwhelmed, overstimulated, and overanalyzing what the sword could do. Marisol wanted to know if she would be able to do something as big as fix her country, or at least fix her school. Jerrold wondered if he could get closer to his true identity. And Dante thought over and over about Martha.

Chapter 12

THE THREE FOUND THEIR way out of the cave in half the time it took to find the sword. The tape and camera crews were cleared away like a great wind had swept them aside. Marisol wasn't as surprised as Jerrold and Dante, but all three counted themselves lucky.

Not far away they could hear voices chatting and clambering, so they knew that they had exited at the perfect time. The woods of the Deschutes were warmer, literally. They had been inside the cave all night, puzzling and searching.

"The air's warm," Dante said. "It must be noon or something."

"I think you're right," Marisol said. In the light of the woods she took a shawl out of her backpack and wrapped the blade within its folds. She stuffed it back into her bag. The top half of the blade stuck out like an overly-thick radio antenna.

Dante eyed it carefully as she did so.

"So back to Bend, then?" Jerrold asked.

"I guess so," Marisol said. "I don't know about you guys, but I really need to unwind. A park sounds good. That work?"

"Like before? Yeah that's fine," Dante chugged forward along the path.

The troupe hitched a ride back into town at the trail head. The news vans and media had died down—some were still stationed out, paninis and coffees half-eaten and steaming, but nobody seemed to be around. The sword knew all about that, and Marisol had a hunch.

"You kids were camping, huh? On a Tuesday?" their old man driver said.

"That's right, yup," Dante said.

"Well great, I love school these days. So counterculture. Oregon, right?"

"That's right, yup."

The Lyft deposited them at Drake Park, their lunch destination from the beginning of their adventure, but it was a much livelier scene this time.

There were three groups of people hanging out, despite it being a Wednesday afternoon. Frisbees of various sizes and weights spun through their air as young-ish adults leapt up to throw and catch the spinning discs. Beards and man buns and thick glasses dotted the crowds.

"Being an adult seems pretty easy," Jerrold said as the three of them sat down at their same rusty picnic table. He took off his Asic shoes and set them on the table; Marisol took off her fleece and left it as she walked to the water's edge. Dante lay down by their table to stretch. Marisol lay the sword down next to him, just beside his ribs.

"You aren't from around here!" a voice called out to her.

The red alert went off in Marisol's brain. Her eyes darted toward the entrance to the parking lot, they darted toward the water—she entered survival mode.

"Sorry, not in, like, a bad way."

A boy sat down next to her. He was taller than her, and looked about the same age. His coat was brown and too warm for a day like today. It looked like a ranchero's uniform.

"I'm Rodrigo Rozenberg," he said.

"I'm Marisol," she said. "What do you want?"

"Oh, just to say, 'Hey.' My friends and I are over a few tables away. It's a half-day so we just got some La Croix and brought a soccer ball."

"That's great," Marisol said. "*Hey.*"

He laughed. A little splash *splashed* a few feet in front of them, a mystery thing in the water.

"*Hey,*" he smiled. "If you and your friends want to hang out we'll be over there!"

"Alright," Marisol said.

Rodrigo stood and walked off toward his pals. Marisol was perplexed. She didn't know, and certainly didn't trust, Rodrigo. But she liked his name. He could be in her community and she might not even know.

Plus she really liked his smile. And that coat. Even though, she thought, it was too hot to wear.

"Hey guys," Marisol walked back to the table.

Jerrold was texting. Dante had begun to snooze lightly.

"Hey guys," Marisol said. "I'm going to walk over to that table. They have La Croix."

"La What?" Dante asked, his eyes still mostly shut.

"La Croix, like L-a c-r-o-y," Marisol said. "It's like pretend water."

"I'll pretend to be asleep, then," Dante said, smiling and closing his eyes.

"I'll be over in a second, Marisol," Jerrold said, his eyes never leaving the screen.

As Marisol walked over to the table, Jerrold's phone *brrt*ed. It was Toby.

> *Toby: People are pretty worried, Jerrold.*
>
> *Jerrold: I know. I'm sorry. I just don't want to be sorry for taking this time for myself.*
>
> *Toby: That's okay. You don't have to be. What are you doing?*
>
> Jerrold's fingers crushed the screen as fast as they could.
>
> *Jerrold: Exploring. Oregon, yes, but mostly myself. I feel pretty different. And I just saw a lot of myself for the first time, like really fast.*
>
> *Toby: Wow. How?*
>
> *Jerrold: I don't know. Something happened and I can't stop thinking about myself with new eyes, and new hair. things like that.*
>
> *Toby: Sounds scary.*
>
> *Jerrold: It's good. Scary but good. Any ways I should go.*
>
> *Toby: Okay. I miss you a lot.*
>
> *Jerrold: <3*
>
> *Toby: <3*

Jerrold ignored the calls and texts he saw piling up like dirty laundry and stowed his phone in his back pocket. The smile he kept plastered to his face. He got up to join Marisol.

Rodrigo wasn't kidding about La Croix. There were five cases of the canned water, different flavors like baseball cards. Sported between the boxes like dandelions were packets of cookies and Twizzlers.

"Jerrold!" Marisol was sitting by Rodrigo, her knees at a perfect right angle from the table to the bench. Rodrigo waved. Three girls and four more guys were standing around, kicking a soccer ball back and forth and dancing to someone's Spotify. But Jerrold realized he really had no idea if they were boys or girls.

"Hey Marisol," Jerrold said, a nervous smile spreading. "How we doin' gang?"

Rodrigo laughed.

"I like this kid! That's awesome. 'How we doin' gang?' Lawl."

One of the kids tossed Jerrold a grapefruit flavored La Croix.

"Pamplemousse? French words are hilarious," Jerrold said.

A few more kids laughed. Someone kicked him the ball. He trapped it and sent it back their way. With the music chiming behind them, it was a good escape. It didn't matter that underneath Marisol's bag she had an actual sword wrapped in a shawl made by her mother.

"Can I text you sometime?" Rodrigo asked.

"Yeah, sure," Marisol said.

"Dope, cool. Where you from?"

"Oakland."

"Is it cool there?"

"Pretty cool, but it's kind of a hard time."

Rodrigo grabbed a handful of Twizzlers and dropped a few in Marisol's hands. They chewed the plastic-y delights in the afternoon warmth.

"How's that?" he asked.

"You read the news right? It's a really hard time."

"Oh, yeah," he said. "My family in Brazil is having a conniption. It's really confusing to get my cousins up here now."

Marisol almost choked on her candy.

"Mine too! I mean," she said. "It's just a hard time. But you get it I guess."

"Yeah. I try to enjoy while I can."

Marisol thought about that.

"I don't really agree," she heard herself say. "I mean, shouldn't you *do* something if you feel like there's a problem?"

"What am I supposed to do?"

"A lot of things. I like to help out at my youth center. There's a lot of really pretty plants that I take care of. My brothers meet me there sometimes and we work together."

Rodrigo swallowed his last chunks of licorice.

"But what does that *do*? Like your flowers are making a big change?"

"Yeah," she said. "I think they are. And I know I'm good at coding, and I really like pottery, and I think that helps."

"That's cool," Rodrigo said. "I dig that. Want to play some soccer?"

"We better get going," Marisol said. "Maybe another time."

Rodrigo smiled and nodded. Marisol smiled, too. She called out to Jerrold and he made a deep bow, a deep curtsy, pretended to throw peanuts in his face, and jogged over. He smuggled a can of the funny sounding 'Pampel-moose' along with him.

They roused Dante, and he was very hungry. They decided that they had better get some food in them, and they could only think of one good place.

Their next Lyft took them through the simple Bend roads. The sword sat at their feet, still poking out of Marisol's bag; they told the driver it was an antique cane.

They pulled up to The Ore-gone-ian and it was looking about the same as when they had left. It was busier, though, with at least thirty people in and out of the café, lining the streets. Jerrold saw the peanut butter cookies in their hands.

"Ooh," Jerrold said. "I gotta get another cookie. Or ten."

"I'm sure Howard is slammed," Dante said.

"Let's just head in," Marisol said. With the sword in her bag, she was feeling confident again.

"Aight," Dante murmured.

They finagled their way through Patagonia and Marmot-sporting trendsetters of the PNW. Inside it was even more hectic. Howard was whipping up mochas and cortados behind the counter as an even older woman was busy taking orders. The two would dance between each other to fulfill tiny requests and bring out drinks. The three sat on a big leather couch at the back and waited.

About thirty minutes later it was managed. The two behind the counter sighed a big sigh before they spotted the traveling "fish."

"Ah!" the woman yelled. "You must be Dante, Jerrold, and Marisol! Come here, come here!"

She slammed the counter and the three walked forward. She had rings along her fingers and a wonderfully pointed face; her smile told a story all on its own.

"Howie told me about you three," she said. Her eyes were as dazzling as Howard's—a pristine and icy blue. "I'm Shanna."

"Hey Shanna," Jerrold said. "What's a guy gotta do to get a peanut butter cookie around here, huh?? Wocka wocka!"

Shanna doubled over and Howard shook his head as he handed Jerrold a cookie. Dante snickered, but Marisol wanted answers.

"We went in the cave. It was amazing, but really confusing. I found a sword."

"I gained powers," Jerrold said while spitting cookie on himself.

"And I didn't," Dante said, spouting a wry grin.

"Wocka wocka indeed," Howard smiled. He wiped his worn hands on his Carhart shirt, ridding himself of coffee stuff. "Let's go out to the patio, fishies."

Shanna took a plate of cookies with them to the garden wonderland. Howard and Shanna sat on one side of the green and black table, their hands on each other's thighs. The other three sat down across from them.

"What was it like?" Howard asked. "Brewer's Yawn, that is."

"It was a puzzle, for sure. It got so tight in spots we had to crawl. Then it was full of these aggressive rat things called kobolds. It was weird as hell," Marisol spewed. "The only way we got through was because Jerrold could somehow see things in the dark."

"Really, Jerrold?" Shanna asked, eyebrows raising.

"Kind of. It wasn't seeing, though, not really. It was more like I could picture it all in front of me. Like my mind made a map, and I was reading it."

"And the sword," Marisol added.

"A sword?" Howard asked. "From Westeros kind of sword? Wait—*the* sword?"

"I dunno, really," Marisol said. She took her pack and unzipped the top, removing the bundle. Once unwrapped, this quartz's shine blew Howard and Shanna's gorgeous eyes out of the water.

"My word," Shanna said. "You have *got* to be careful with something like that."

"It felt like I could shape my thoughts. I knew in the cave I needed to keep us safe—to light up the cave, to get rid of the kobolds," Marisol sort of shrugged. "It was a lot to handle."

"Just like the Yawn had come out of the earth, raising and molding. . .manifesting," Howard muttered. "That's fascinating!"

The five sat in the back and no one said anything for a moment, all eyes on the ancient artifact. It wasn't some kind of "Lord of the Rings" thing—it was just an exceptionally beautiful weapon. The edge along it looked so sharp that it could split the tiniest needle, in the tiniest haystack, right down the middle.

"So what are you going to do now? With the sword?"

"I don't know," Marisol said. "I guess we should practice with it a bit."

"Like cutting stuff with it?" Dante asked.

"No, like making things with it. Howard, where might be a good place for us to try it out?"

"I don't see why they couldn't stay at our place, eh Shanna?" Howard looked over at his partner.

"I don't see why not at all."

The two closed up The Ore-gone-ian early and led the three to their Subaru Outback parked around the corner.

"Don't you think it's weird they're so okay with us being away from home?" Jerrold whispered to Dante.

"I think they're probably real familiar with this kind of thing, Jerry," Dante said.

The three hopped in the back of the crammed, teal car. The seats were covered with dog hair, which meant immediately that the three of them were covered with dog hair.

As they drove out of town they saw a small school. Marisol recognized what it looked like—it was impoverished. A dry patch of grass on the side of the building was the only thing the children had to play with. Big stretches of pavement were their only playthings. Some kids were in a semi-circle in the back.

"Wait," Marisol said. "Stop the car."

Howard pulled over as Marisol unbuckled herself. She flung open the car door and ran to the chain link fence surrounding the school. She was still looking when Jerrold walked up to her.

"What do you see, Jerrold?"

"It looks like five kids are probably bullying that one kid," Jerrold said. "That sucks."

"They don't have any outlet," Marisol said. "No resources."

Marisol took the sword out of its sheath. Jerrold stepped back toward the car. Howard, Shanna, and Dante sat in the car watching. None of them could quite tell what was going to happen.

Marisol's eyes went bright and the wind whipped around her fleece as she started channeling the sword's energies. Jerrold was flabbergasted at what he began to see.

Grass began to sprout out of the patchy deadness of the schoolyard. It was like some enormous caretaker had laid turf over the whole place, and greenery kept on blooming. Hydrangeas and tulips in planters lining the chain link fence suddenly materialized out of nothing.

The kids on the black top turned their gaze to the yard and their jaws dropped. One little girl threw her hands to her head like she'd seen an elephant fly by.

Marisol grunted, a bit of sweat coming from her brow, and continued.

With a tremendous crack, the earth began to issue forth metal bars and plastic chutes. Growing like vines from the freshly planted grass came monkey bars, swings, and a complete set of jungle gyms. An impish yellow slide, the perfect size for the kids in the yard, bloomed into existence.

An oasis of joy flooded the once barren school. Marisol fell towards the concrete, Jerrold just barely catching her fall.

The children were clearly shocked, but the littlest one, the one who was being mocked in the center of the semi-circle, went boldly into the new world. Within minutes all six kids were playing together like there had never been anything other than an idyllic playground for them all to enjoy.

Dante helped Jerrold sit Marisol in the backseat.

"Oh my god," Howard's hand was plastered to his forehead. "It's unreal. The power of that thing. And her power as well." Dante looked at Howard, then at Marisol and Jerrold who were now getting into the car. He nodded silently, thinking.

"We better get out of here," Shanna said. "Before someone realizes that a 16-year-old girl just brandished a sword at Bend's worst elementary school."

"I think it just became the best," Howard said. He threw the car in drive and the five sped off.

Marisol was feeling less groggy a few John Denver songs into the ride. She told them all how she felt compelled to offer the kids something that she never had at her own school. They said that was of course generous of her, but really Marisol, who knew you could do *that*?

She just folded her arms and looked out the window, a tiny smile on her face.

The roads outside Bend were suburban for a bit, and flat, but as they snaked into the edges of the forest, they saw some houses removed from the road dotting the periphery. Howard slowed the car and lolled the wheel to the left.

"Casa de Shannibald," she smiled. "Shanna and Archibald, aka my dad. This place has been in my family for a while."

"Is your dad here?!" Jerrold asked.

"Oh no," Shanna said. "My dad died a long time ago."

"Oh," Jerrold said. "Sorry."

Shanna looked over her shoulder and smiled.

"It's okay, Jerrold," Shanna said. "If my dad had been the guy to achieve immortality, he probably would have spent a thousand years just watching Lifetime movies and eating Ben & Jerry's."

They both snickered, and Marisol snorted out a laugh. Dante thought about Martha, and a tiny smile frosted on his lips.

The place was as idiosyncratic as their café. But ten times as beautiful. Firs lined the road like tree guardians to their royal chariot. The house was a rambler with a well-crafted deck, and one could see well-planted gardens behind the sky-blue home.

Lawn gnomes and flamingos were planted intermittently across the yard. It seemed like their home wouldn't be complete without tchotchke.

"You like it?" Howard asked.

"It's so whimsical," Marisol said.

"Like a mini-golf course," Jerrold said.

"Do you have a lint roller?" Dante asked.

Shanna took Dante and Jerrold inside when they parked, and Howard and Marisol went around back. The afternoon light was fading fast, and the trees seemed to reduce the light even quicker. Howard showed Marisol their blackberry bushes, and explained how even though to some it was a wild weed, they truly cherished the plant.

"It's not easy being a fish and it's not easy being a weed," Howard said, crinkling the plant in his hands. "So Shanna and I like to harbor what we can and help where we're able."

"I understand," Marisol said. "I was bullied by some kids at school. That's why I went on this crazy journey in the first place."

"I'm sorry to hear that. Do you miss your family?"

"Yes," she said.

"Then you'll be okay," Howard patted her on the back. "If you didn't, then we might have to worry."

Advice coming from Howard didn't feel patronizing, or unwelcome. He seemed like someone she could learn to trust, and that was new. He described all the dogs who lived there—six total—and how from the smallest terrier to the biggest Labrador they were each unique persons with their own personalities.

"Come on inside, you can meet 'em," he said.

Inside there was more tchotchke than she could have ever imagined. It looked like Jerrold and Dante were just as real as the rag dolls and snow globes that surrounded them—so not real at all. If something didn't look artificial, it looked like it really didn't belong there. More apt to be found at a garage sale than in someone's kitchen.

"Tea?" Shanna asked. "We have kombucha, too."

"Of course you do," Dante smirked.

"Let's take a look at it, Marisol," Howard interrupted. "The sword, I mean."

"I'd love tea," Marisol said. "And sure."

She unwrapped the artifact again and laid it on the table. Howard brought out his journal and began to compare the drawing to the blade.

"That's it alright. Whatever my great-grandpappy and the Kalapuya fella saw, it was the same as this. The jewel encrusted in the blade is the same. And we've seen what you can do with it."

"That's right," Marisol said.

"The whole town has seen, by the way," Shanna said.

She walked over to the table with her smart phone in hand. The Bulletin, Bend's local rag, had released a still-updating digital news release recounting how an enormous playground had been gifted to the school by some generous donor. The crazy thing, the story said, was how fast the mysterious benefactor set about constructing it.

"'I wasn't aware of such a donation,'" Shanna read. "'But I know all of Piedmont Elementary is glad to have received it,' Principal Buchmeier says. Can you believe it?"

"How else do they explain something like that? I wouldn't know how to," Dante said. "Someone should do something like that for *my* school. Kids might stop doing so many drugs."

"Well we gotta find out if it works for the others, then," Howard said. "Jerrold! Come on over!"

Jerrold walked across the carpeted floor and onto the slightly raised kitchen flooring. A labradoodle named Tiger rubbed against him, coming up to his hip. He stroked her snout, and got his hand wet.

"I'm afraid," he said. "I don't know if this is a part of what I'm supposed to do with it. I was the seer."

"The sword could help with those powers," Howard said. "Why don't you try?"

"Don't make him do anything he doesn't want to, Howie," Shanna said, bringing a Jasmine tea over to Marisol. The cup was hot to the touch.

"I can try," Jerrold said. "How did you do it, Marisol?"

"I just held the hilt, like you told me to in the cave. I gripped it hard and felt strong, and everything I needed to have happen sort of just happened." Remembering then, "You told me, 'Don't forget who you are.'"

He looked at her, nodding his head slowly. "Okay, so like this?" Jerrold took the hilt in his hands and pressed together, like he was pushing a wish into his palms. Right away the atmosphere in the room sunk, so much that Shanna gripped the counter for balance. Jerrold's eyes glowed a bright yellow and pink and his feet dug into the wood.

In a flash, fifty peanut butter cookies materialized on the table, like someone had punched in the os and 1s, with dashes of brown sugar and peanuts, to create the treats. They rattled to the table like dice finishing their spin.

"Cookies, Jerry?" Dante asked. "Really?!"

But Jerrold couldn't hear anyone in the room. The power was still coursing through him, they could see it. Outside the black berry bush began to produce fat, juicy berries. They became so ripe that they swelled and popped just seconds after blossoming.

The dog's bowls in the garage filled to the brim with food, big shanks of lamb, and a dozen packets of Jasmine tea fell onto the table in front of Shanna, who gave out a shriek.

"How long will he go on like this?" Howard asked over the dull whushing in the room.

"Marisol finished up right quick," Dante blurted, "but she was doing something specific. Jerry is just experimenting. Who knows?"

A few more flowers outside took full bloom, and the fridge got suddenly stocked with fruits and vegetables, before the power seemed to ooze out of Jerrold. He collapsed, and the sword fell to his feet with a *clang*.

"My word," Shanna sang. "It's like you said."

"Pretty nuts, right?" Dante said. "Let me try."

"That may have been enough for now," Howard said.

"Oh come on! I don't have powers? I don't get to practice with the sword? This is crap!"

"Easy, Dante. It'll happen in time. Don't rush anything like this," Howard said. "If my great grand-pappy was right, then this thing has a lot of power. Plenty, I'm sure, to share."

"Yeah, it's got to happen as it's got to happen," Marisol shrugged.

"Easy for you to say. You got to save the day. What important thing have I done other than leave my parents? And mess everything up?"

Dante slammed the door as he went outside. He fiddled with his phone in the drive way, the big trees watching over him like guardians. No new messages on Instagram. No new texts. The last one he had from his mom read:

"We want you to be safe. Please come home <3"

He ughed and stuffed it back in his pocket. Nothing for him to do. No one for him to be that hasn't already been tried out.

"Dante," a voice called from the void.

He looked around and saw nothing. Nobody was around him—they had let him stew outside. But he had heard that voice as though it were just over his shoulder.

"I'm not over your shoulder—I'm still in Brewer's Yawn."

"The cave? Who are you?"

"It's not so important just yet," the voice smiled. "It's important that you *do* practice with the sword. You could do amazing things with that sword, Dante. You could bring back Martha."

Dante felt a bead of sweat arc his neck. His gulp sounded like dynamite.

"How do you know that?"

"I know the sword well, Dante," the voice said. "We have a history. You need a chance to practice, that's all. You're the oldest! It's only fair."

"That's how I feel," Dante said, confiding in the voice. "It's a crappy deal. How else am I supposed to prove that I can make a change, too?"

"Take the sword," the voice spat.

"What?"

"Take it! And make the change *you* want to see," the voice hummed.

"I can't take it from Marisol and Jerrold," Dante said. "They're my friends."

"Two strangers you met at a bus stop in Oregon are your *friends*? You might have lower standards than I thought, Dante," the voice chided.

"Hey, up yours," Dante stood and went back inside. The voice hushed. He stormed past the four in the kitchen and ruffled through his bags for a pair of shorts. After changing in the bathroom, he took off on a run down the dirt path.

The remaining four stood, perplexed, in the kitchen.

"He's got to relax! We've made an amazing discovery here!" Howard said, resting his hands on his hips.

"We made the discovery, Howard," Marisol reminded him. "But we couldn't have done it without you."

"It's true! But what are we really going to do with it?" Jerrold had been sitting on the couch, gaining his strength by stuffing more cookies in his mouth. Or that's what he told himself, any ways.

"You've only just begun experimenting with it," Shanna said. "Maybe the best thing to do is just keep practicing? It's true Dante needs to test his mettle, and maybe with some more regular practice from you two, you really could do some pretty uh-mazing things. That school was no joke."

"I'll caution again," Howard said, crossing the kitchen toward Shanna. "That my great-grandpappy and that Klamath man didn't drop it down a well for all of its world-changing-ly good stuff. They rid the world of it. But Shanna's right, with some practice maybe it can be the thing this world needs right now."

"Like Superman," Jerrold said.

"Sort of, sure," Howard sighed.

The rest of the afternoon was spent with Jerrold and Marisol periodically taking turns using the sword. Jerrold was only ever able to make small miracles—flowers growing and food being replenished—but Marisol was making real progress. She brought fallen trees in the yard twenty feet into the air. She formed a few smaller Brewer's Yawns along the dirt path—caves that fit all four of them. She changed the color of the house to any color someone could think of, pink, orange, even seafoam green, and did it without asking anyone what color they wanted. She just knew.

"Marisol, that's very impressive," Shanna said.

Howard and Jerrold had gone inside to make sure the dogs weren't eating themselves to death, and Shanna sat on the porch.

"I know," she said. "But I want to do more with it."

"What do you mean? You've only just begun experimenting with that crazy thing."

Marisol came to sit down with Shanna. She trusted her, even though she'd only known her for a few hours.

"Yeah. But don't worry, you're right that we're just learning how it works."

"It's exciting though, isn't it? All of that creativity flowing from your fingers. The power of maybe."

Marisol looked at Shanna and saw in her face Mrs. Neuschwander—a woman who understood what it was like to be told 'no' and made to feel less. And said *that's enough.*

"How long have you and Howard known each other?"

"Oh about twenty years, I guess," Shanna smiled. "He's a handful. But we really get along. My last partner was as boring as could be, and not very nice, either. Howard and I have been adventuring together since he took me out for a hike in the woods here."

"Did you ever have kids?"

"No. We decided dogs, a business, and each other was plenty," Shanna winked.

"That's great," Marisol said. "I don't think anyone my age has anything that normal going on."

"Normal? All this? With magic swords and angry elf rat things?"

"No, a relationship that seems so, like, friendly," Marisol said. "I've never really dated. It freaks me out."

"It'll happen when it's supposed to happen," Shanna said. "Don't think about it too much, if you can help it. You seem to be doing just fine all on your own."

"Thanks Shanna," Marisol "I think you're right."

Marisol stood and smiled at Shanna, who smiled right back. They walked into the house together and started talking about organic tamales as they made pozole for dinner.

Dante came back in and sheepishly apologized for "freaking out." No one minded, and he helped set the table. For the night, the five of them were each other's family. Jerrold worried about what his parents would think if they knew how much he loved this—dining and joking with complete strangers. Marisol and Dante already knew their families would be appalled. Howard, Shanna, and their six dogs all just enjoyed the company.

They all had a copious fill of pozole, and even the dogs were allowed to slurp up some leftovers.

As Shanna and Howard did the dishes, Marisol whispered to Dante:

"Do you think they've called our parents?"

"It's possible," Dante said. "But you could just use the sword to make them go away if they *did* show up." Marisol thought for a moment that she saw a strange light in his eyes.

"I wouldn't want to do that!"

"Just kiddin'," Dante said. "But, really, I'm not too worried. Let's just get some good sleep tonight. Last night was pretty over the top. I think we all need to relax for a night and we can figure out more about the sword tomorrow."

"Good idea. I think I'll keep it in my room tonight."

"Great."

Chapter 13

JERROLD AND DANTE SHARED the living room, and Marisol was given the guest room. It was decorated intensely. One couldn't move very far without bumping into a snow globe from the 1977 World's Fair or a collector's Beanie Baby from 2001. The covers on the bed looked more like a crochet or macramé project than a blanket. It was about 10 o'clock when they finally finished talking and cleaning up from the day.

The three travelers brushed their teeth in their pajamas side-by-side-by-side. They appeared for all the world to be triplets.

"Good night, Marisol," Shanna and Howard came by Marisol's room as she was reading in bed.

"Thank you for everything, again, good night," Marisol said. She turned to the vintage bedside lamp and pulled the gold beads down, shutting it off. The room clicked instantly into darkness.

"Do you boys need anything?" Shanna asked Dante and Jerrold as they finished setting up the living room for the two. Dante was scrolling through his phone as he sat on an inflatable air mattress, and Jerrold was snuggling further into the couch cushions that he was stretched out upon.

"I think we're alri –"

"I'm not a boy," Jerrold said.

"Oh?" Shanna and Howard paused what they had begun to busy themselves with.

"I don't really know; I think I'm just going to call myself somewhere in-between for now."

"Well do either of you need anything?" Shanna asked.

"I think we're alright," Dante finished.

"Yeah, thanks though!" Jerrold said, pulling his covers tighter around himself.

"Glad to hear it," Shanna said.

Dante and Jerrold turned out the light after the two adults had gone off to bed. One Jack Russel Terrier and a German Shorthaired Pointer, Jake and Goose respectively, slept just next to them in front of a faux fireplace.

"Did you mean that, Jerry?" Dante asked. "The whole 'boy' thing?"

"Yeah. Yeah, I think so. I got to see a lot of things while I was in the cave, and now that I've used the sword I've seen even more. Mostly about myself."

"Yeah?"

"I think I'm starting to get why my life in Eugene stresses me out so much," Jerrold turned over. "It's confusing. I'm going to try and get some sleep, 'kay Dante?"

"Yeah for sure, Jerry. Sleep tight."

"Thanks for asking."

"Yeah," Dante turned over. "Of course."

Once Jerrold was really sleeping, maybe twenty minutes later, Dante heard the voice again.

"Why didn't you get a chance to practice with the sword today, Dante?"

"Leave me alone," Dante whispered.

"Doesn't it seem odd?" the voice sounded like a bit of leather dunked in honey.

"No. I went on a run. So I was gone."

"They didn't even *offer* for you to try it out, though," the voice cooed.

"Who cares? I'll try it tomorrow."

"You've already decided to try it out tonight, or so I thought."

Dante gulped that explosive gulp again.

"How did you know that?"

"I don't *know* it. You just seem—tense."

"Can you see me? Or can you read my thoughts?"

"That's really not the important issue, Dante. The issue is the *sword*. It's so dark, Marisol probably won't even notice."

Dante stood up. The house was silent, a graveyard.

"I know that. I just didn't know *you* knew that."

The voice said nothing. Dante continued with his plan.

It really wasn't fair the way they had treated him today, and he just wanted a chance to see what he could do. He wasn't going to do anything enormous. Not yet. He just wanted to feel that rush, too, the same rush that they got to have.

He stepped over the snoring dogs and down the hall. Each step he took was as gentle as he could muster, and he twisted the guest room's door knob the very same.

Marisol snored a little, and Dante was grateful because it meant he knew for sure that she was sleeping. The shawl-wrapped sword was just under her bed, a little bit sticking out from under the cherry-colored frame.

Dante's fingers wrapped around the cloth and pulled it from beneath the bed. It felt tense—like Marisol could stir at any second from her sleep. But she wouldn't have. She slept a deep sleep because she trusted everyone in the house.

Once he had the sword in his hands, Dante felt horrible. But he took it outside all the same, the gentle clinking of the screen door rattling in his brain. His anxiety was at an all-time high, but he had his mind made up.

"Terrific," the rich voice hummed. "You know what to do."

"Don't talk to me like that! I'm just practicing. I should get a chance to practice, too."

"That's right. It's only fair. What will you do first, Dante?"

He had walked into the garden and found himself amongst growing and sleeping things, the cool air making his cold sweat even colder.

"I want to bring Martha back."

Dante unwrapped the sword and tossed the shawl aside. He planted himself between a few rows of brush, and admired the sword in one hand. Even in near-total darkness, the gem looked mystical, bright.

"Phenomenal," the voice said. "And this is only the beginning."

Dante stopped.

"What's only the beginning?" his mind raced quickly through a thousand scenarios. "What are you talking about?"

The voice paused. Total silence in the garden.

"Bringing back the dead. It's the first of many wonderful things you'll do with the Native's power," the voice said. "You're so passionate. I know I can trust you, Dante."

"I don't know what Native you mean," Dante said. He dropped the sword. "But I don't like the way you're putting it. Bringing back the dead?"

"Making your whims truth is an overwhelming concept," the voice assured. "You'll come to terms in time. Grab the sword."

Dante reached for it. The thousand scenarios turned into a million. He pictured Martha's hands, green nail polish and all, meeting his as he picked up the sword. He imagined them falling apart, bones jutting out helter skelter.

"No," Dante sat down like he had been shoved over. "No, no, no. I made a mistake. I better go inside. I'm being hasty."

"NO!" the voice crashed inside his head.

"Gah! What the hell?"

"No," the voice spoke. "Do as you're told, Dante. If having her in your life is so important to you, then do it now."

"Who the hell are you?! Leave me alone!"

Dante got up to grab the sword and run inside.

"The king will not be denied," the voice spoke. "I know you'll do what's right for Martha, Dante."

Chapter 14

HE SLAMMED THE DOOR as he flew inside. Tears came down his face as he hurried to wake up Jerrold. All the dogs started barking and soon the whole house was awake again.

Dante couldn't get out a sentence. His head felt full and thick like in Tacoma, like he couldn't speak for himself or for anyone. And like he couldn't do anything right.

"It's alright, Dante," Shanna cooed. "Take your time. Howie, get some cookies out."

Jerrold and Marisol sat in their pajamas at the table with Shanna and Dante. They were silent, hoping that Dante was alright.

"I took the sword," Dante sputtered after some time.

"I noticed," Marisol said. "I thought it might have been you."

"Why, Dante? And why, Marisol?! Dante's our friend!" Jerrold said.

"Because he never got to use it today," Marisol said.

"I," Dante said. "I wanted to try it out. I'm sorry for taking it without asking, I was just overwhelmed."

"It's alright," Marisol said. "I didn't think you did anything wrong. It's just as much yours as it is mine."

"That's true," Jerrold said. "It's all of ours."

"But someone else wants it," Dante said. "Someone was in my head talking to me."

"What?" Howard came to the table with a plate full of cookies, thawing from their storage in the freezer. Jerrold took one and wolfed it away, then grabbed another.

"It was some voice," Dante wiped away some tears. "It called itself a 'king.'"

Howard drummed his fingers on the table exactly once before turning around and heading back toward the back of the house. Shanna shrugged and grabbed a cookie for herself. The walrus-mustachioed man returned to the kitchen and laid the old journal on the table. He licked his thumb and began turning pages.

"There was an awakening for many of you in Brewer's Yawn," Howard said. "Jerrold's sight. Marisol's power. And, though I hoped it wouldn't be so, apparently for some elder being as well."

He stopped turning the pages. A rough charcoal sketch approximating the sword was smeared on the page. There was a big black circle with smaller red circles inside. It looked like someone crossed a house fly with a boulder.

"'It called itself," Howard read. "King Karrabad. And it spoke to me as the Chinook fellow and I carried the sword to the well. It told me of riches and control, and of its shackles in the earth. He showed me himself and it was a horror.' That's all that's really written."

"That's it?" Shanna asked.

"Well, no," Howard said. "It sounds like they didn't interact with him much, though."

"Should we be worried? I didn't see him when I was inside the cave," Jerrold said.

"Yes we should be worried! He was saying all kinds of messed up things," Dante said.

"Let's try and get some sleep tonight, fishes," Howard said. "And tomorrow we can use the sword to close Brewer's Yawn. It seems like the time has come for that geological burp to be un-burped."

"Okay," Marisol said. "Buenos noches."

"Good night everyone," Shanna said. "See you in bed, Howie."

Jerrold went to hop back in bed, but Dante sat at the table. Howard smiled and looked at him for a while.

"It's going to be hard to get to sleep," Dante said. "Knowing he can reach inside my head like that."

"Yeah," Howard said. "So far it sounds like he isn't doing anything *too* devious. What does he really want any ways, I wonder."

The two sat in silence for a second. Howard looked up and saw Dante's forlorn expression.

"Hey, I've got a trick for ya. You an anxious guy, Dante?"

Dante looked at him with eyes narrowed.

"Maybe," Dante said. "I think about things a lot."

"I had a hunch," Howard said. "Try this on for size. Close your eyes."

Dante did.

"Picture a wide open field. Picture a desert with a tornado off in the distance. Picture the beach, with miles and miles of ocean in front of you and nothing else in the world nearby," Howard's eyes were closed too. "Now breathe. Take in one big breath, and let it fill you up, then let it go."

"I keep thinking about King Karrabad. And Martha."

"It's hard. It's a practice. I am still learning every day. But try it out sometime. It can even help with getting to sleep!"

Howard stood up and winked at Dante before heading off to bed. Dante sat and twiddled his fingers at the table for a while. A Dalmatian sat under the table and licked his feet.

After a few more minutes he crawled onto the couch again.

He saw Tacoma from a bird's eye view. He saw the waterfront, and the traffic going along the interstate. He saw the South End where Martha had died, and his house where his family was dying. Then he breathed.

It didn't feel quite as bad.

Chapter 15

IN THE MORNING THE three of them had vegan oatmeal. It wasn't their favorite, none of them were much accustomed to the Oregon culture, but Jerrold assured them that it was a lot like normal oatmeal but a lot healthier. Dante said he really didn't care about that, but Marisol just ate and said gracias.

"Alright," Howard rubbed his hands together. "After everything that happened yesterday, I think we know what we have to do."

Everyone looked at him, not knowing at *all* what he might mean by that.

"Dante has to try out the sword!"

Dante grinned, and Marisol and Jerrold nodded. The five of them walked outside and into the garden, which was beginning to feel more like a dojo than a place to pick radishes. Marisol handed Dante the sword and he unwrapped it.

In his hands it felt lighter than it did last night. He kept picturing the waterfront of Tacoma, the Thea-Foss Waterway and the gentle stillness it maintains when you're just trying to get through traffic. He breathed slowly.

The air around him began to stiffen before popping; electrodes in his body were charging and rising. He dug his palms into the hilt of the sword and focused on changing the world. Focused on overcoming the drug abuse issues that terrorized his home. Focused on healing the rift in his family. Focused on making a change.

But nothing happened. As soon as the air began to crack it relaxed, and the power inside him seemed to dissipate. Nothing changed. He let the sword fall to the ground.

"I don't get it," Dante said.

"Maybe you're just not made to use a sword," Shanna said. "They're pretty intense weapons. There are lots of other things to use besides a sword."

"They only *have* a sword, love," Howard said.

"I know, I know," Shanna said. "Just food for thought. I'm going to get some tea ready. Chamomile, Dante?"

"Yeah, sure," Dante said. The soothing thoughts were gone and he felt insignificant again. He felt tears welling in his eyes. Then he felt Marisol's hand on his shoulder.

"It's alright," she said. "Who knows why the sword does what it does? It's not your fault."

"Yeah," Jerrold said. "I think it really has a thing for Marisol. You and I have different powers."

"What's my power?" Dante asked.

"No se," Marisol said. "And that's pretty cool. Think of all your potential."

Dante smiled a little bit, but asked if they could do something else. All three walked back inside, wrapping the sword in its homemade sheath again, and sat at the table for tea. After a few minutes of drinking their beverages, they were still trying to find a way to break the tension.

"Anything fun to do on your property, Shanna?" Jerrold asked. "Non-magical related fun?"

"Hm," Shanna said. "You could head to the Secret Place."

All three spun around in their chairs, their eyes lighting up.

"There are some willow trees, like a glen, down to the east side of the house. We used to go there with Howard's niece and nephew when they were young."

All three raced out of their chairs. It felt good to take their minds off of the last few days, how crazy it all had been since leaving home. No one had checked their phones yet, knowing there would be dozens of messages and texts from home. They left them locked away in their bags.

They knew they were getting closer when the ground started to get mushy and soft. A few of the dogs ran with them for a while, but turned back after seeing just how far the kids wanted to go.

Big hanging nests of willow tree branches arced across each other in front of them. It was like a floral gate, an ancient door to access some wonderful harbor. Marisol pushed her hand through some of the branches and winged her arms apart to make a space.

"Wow," she said. "It's so peaceful."

There was a tire swing hanging from the biggest tree trunk. It must have been a tractor tire, it was so big and tough looking. It was suspended like someone could have just been using it, even though they knew this place hadn't had a visitor in a very long time. They were entirely alone, except for some tiny starlings in a nest in the trees, and some frogs in the creek.

"Can you believe what's going on in our lives?!" Jerrold said. "I mean, three days ago I was just a confused kid at a confusing school. Now I'm an oracle or something. I'm only now feeling like I can relax for a second. Still pretty confused, but that's okay, too? I think."

"And I'm a sorceress, or a bruja, or something," Marisol pushed Jerrold on the tire swing. She thought about the little doll in her bag and smiled.

"And I'm still Dante," Dante said. "But I feel a lot better. Than when I was in Tacoma, any ways."

He told them both about how he and Howard had sat and talked about ways to breathe, to clear space in his mind.

"That's amazing, Dante," Jerrold said. "I wish I had done that at school one time. I was so nervous about my dad, and my classmates, I just clammed up. I *bombed*, as my fellow comics might call it."

They laughed, Marisol snorting. She thought about how sometimes when it seems like you can't clear your mind, maybe that's the best time. She thought about the bullies in Oakland, how they made her feel so weak and stupid. How next time she might just try picturing absolutely nothing and see if that wouldn't help.

Jerrold started doing impressions. It was like they were at a talent show, and he was the emcee and the performers. Marisol and Dante both lost it when he started doing an impression of Mike Wozawski from Monsters, Inc. They felt the laughs ring throughout their whole bodies.

Dante was sitting by the bank looking at his reflection. Little tadpoles were emerging from their gelatinous eggs, peeking their heads out for the first time. He twirled a stick in the water, a safe distance away from the tadpoles, and just marveled.

Jerrold joined him, scooting his shoes against the mossy bank. He wondered what it was like for the Chinook people to live here. They had Secret Places all over, he bet.

They heard Miles barking in the distance. It was a frenzied bark like he had gone crazy. In short order the other dogs were yawping and calling. Jerrold dropped his stick and clambered up the river bank. Dante followed, and Marisol hopped off the tire swing to make sure she could help, too.

In a few minutes they were back at the house where they saw Howard and Shanna looking off to the right of the porch. Their eyes were glued to the bottom step. Miles was baring his teeth and barking at whatever they were staring at. Four more dogs were trotting in semi-circles, barking intermittently like stale protestors at city hall.

Dante saw it first—he knew the scene too well.

A kobold was caught in a skunk trap, raking a little spear along the patterned cage. Its battered teeth were covered in plaque and rot, and it smelt like disease. The scales it sported under its crimson eyes were flaking off like a shedding snake.

"My word," Howard said. "This is one of the little things, is it?"

"Yeah," Dante said. "Those things were really messing me up until Marisol fixed everything."

"How did it find us?" Jerrold asked.

"I don't know," Marisol said. "That's really not good."

"They're pretty harmless though," Dante said. "Just knicks and scratches."

"Is that so?" Howard said. "I wonder."

He sounded like a deflating balloon, and turned to walk inside. The screen door jingled like a mortician.

"We caught it," Dante said. "Isn't that lucky? Who knows what it could have done if it were still loose."

"Aw Dante," Shanna said. "This little guy killed our labradoodle. We found her body this morning."

"Tiger?!" Jerrold asked.

Shanna smiled a sad smile.

"Yeah, she was a great pooch. We found her in the garden. That kobold knew where it was going. It knew the sword was real close."

Shanna turned and walked inside, wiping a tear from her eye.

Marisol went over the kobold and into the garden. Jerrold and Dante joined her, and what they all saw made them freeze. Tiger's body was almost unrecognizable. Big chunks of her torso were torn loose, and bite marks ran all along her body. The beautiful fur she used to lay on the porch was stained and matted, like a gross old toy.

Chapter 16

IT WAS GLUM TO be at Casa de Shannibald that afternoon. No one was too sure how to talk to Howie, who was so distraught, and nobody was sure what the kobold coming to their hideaway really meant.

All three of the travelers sat at the kitchen table while Shanna was in the back of the house trying to talk to Howard. Sometimes their voices would rise, but it was a concern thing, not a concerning thing.

"So King Karrabad wants the sword that bad, huh?" Dante said. "He's like a drug addict."

"Maybe," Marisol said. "Or he's just trying to goad us."

"Goat us?" Jerrold asked.

"No, *goad* us," Marisol said.

"I know, I'm just trying to lighten the mood," Jerrold said.

"This is serious, Jerry! Thank god that skunk trap caught the little weirdo," Dante said.

"I know, I just don't know what to do," Jerrold said. "I wish we were at the Secret Place again."

Howard came back out of the back of the house. He marched like the general of an army, and Shanna just smiled and shook her head.

"Alright," he said. "That was horrible. I can't really fathom it just yet. But here's what I think. I like what Jerrold just said."

"About goats?"

"*No*, about hanging out at the Secret Place. A little bit of relaxing today could be just what we need. I want to have a wake for Tiger. She deserved it."

The three smiled and clapped. Shanna told them they should go with her into town to get some party supplies, and that Howie was going to go dig a big plot for Tiger underneath the willows. Beneath the starling nest seemed right, he said.

"Shot gun!" Dante said as they scrambled outside.

They piled into the Subaru as Howard waved from the porch. They played James Taylor as they rolled onto the paved road.

"Hey kids," Shanna said. "You know we would never let anything like that happen to you, right?"

"Well thanks Shanna," Jerrold said. "But you don't have to say that. We know we're runaways."

She tightened her hands on the steering wheel.

"It's important to me," she said. "That you know that Howard and I know how hard this time of life is for you three. And how crazy things have gotten in just a couple of days."

They didn't say anything. There weren't many stop lights on the country roads, but one traffic signal flashed red over and over. Shanna stopped at the light.

"We love you three," she said, looking at them. "And we want to make sure you get home safe. After all of this is over."

"Thank you, Shanna," Marisol said.

She smiled a tight smile and kept driving. It was silence except for James Taylor until they got to the same Safeway they had been to before. They dashed throughout the aisles, grabbing balloons, streamers, Donettes, and Mountain Dew.

"Could we make conchas?" Marisol asked Shanna.

"What's that, sweetie?" Shanna asked.

"It's a sweet bread, we make them for celebrations back in Oakland," she said.

"Could we text your mom for the recipe?" Shanna winked.

"Better not," Marisol said. "But I have it memorized."

"Wow," Shanna said, placing her hands on her hips. "Then you'd better lead the way!"

They grabbed the flour, the sugar, and cinnamon before Shanna said she had all the rest. Dante and Jerrold showed up in the line with their arms full of goodies.

Driving back was less tense. It felt present, like it didn't matter that some underground felon had killed their canine friend. It just didn't matter that some evil king was trying to break free. They were supposed to be having fun, that's what Howard had told them.

When they got back, they spread all the goods out on the counter. Jerrold and Dante toasted the dredges of their tea, celebrating their excellent selections, as Marisol and Shanna got ready to make conchas.

"Anyone want to help?" Shanna asked.

"I'd be happy to," Jerrold said, doing a Jim Carrey. "Dante?"

"I'm going to see if I can help Howard," he said.

The trap was empty when Dante stepped off the porch. Even the little spear was gone, the same kind that they had used to stab Dante in the cave. He looked both ways and saw Howard inside the little shed that rested against the garden like a farmhand taking a breather.

"Hey Howie!" Dante called.

"Oh," Howard called back. "Hold on a moment."

He came out of the shed carrying a shoe box that rocked like a can of shaken soda. Dante had seen something like this before. He followed Howard, who just smiled, as he walked toward the Secret Place. Once inside the grove, they knelt by the bed of the stream. Two of the dogs had followed, Miles the Pyrenees and Deano the Dalmatian, who were yapping like crazy.

"Do you think that's a good idea?" Dante asked.

Howard tied a thick bit of rope around the top of the box.

"Yes," Howard sighed. "Though I don't like to do it. It's the same as when barn cats have too many kittens. There's no good choice. Just the necessary one."

The box squeaked and yelled, somewhere in between a bat and a dinosaur. Little teeth flashed, and eyes peeked, through a hole on the side of the box.

Howard threw the box inside the creek. It wasn't a fast moving creek, but it swept the box away. As soon as it had sunk, that is.

"Sorry you had to be here for this, Dante," Howard said. "I had a harder time getting that thing out of the trap than I thought I might."

"It's okay, I understand what you mean," Dante said. "It's not fun or anything, but it's important. Who knows if it has psychic powers, too— maybe it could bring more to your house."

Howard stood up, his knees brown from the earth. He lent Dante a hand. The two of them called the dogs along a bit more than they needed to as they walked back toward the house. Howard slung an arm around Dante and Dante smiled.

"King Karrabad," Dante said. "He said I could bring my sister back with the sword."

Howard took his arm off of Dante to shove his hands in the pockets of his stained blue jeans.

"Where's your sister?"

"She's gone. She OD'd."

Howard stopped. Dante turned to look at him, and he caught Howard flexing the back of his hand through his eyes. Then he sat down on a felled tree, and patted for Dante to join him.

"Mind talkin' about it?"

"Yes."

Howard looked at his feet. Dante exhaled. He saw the shores of a beach, the heat of a desert.

"Okay. It was at this dumb party. She had been going out with some guy who was way too old and stupid. I had seen her at school that day and she told me she was going, and I said I'd see her there, since I was going, too. That guy wasn't looking out for her at all. He probably gave her the stuff that put her over. But no one could prove it."

Dante moved his shoes so the tears would hit the earth. Howard put his hand on Dante's back.

"I found her in the upstairs of the house. Her eyes were so white."

"So what did you think?"

"About what?"

"Bringing her back," Howard said. "What did you think when he said that?"

Dante mulled the idea over. They stood up and started walking for a moment, underneath some big firs, before stopping again.

"I was scared," Dante said. "I had thought about that, sure, but when I *really* thought about it, I was terrified. I don't think that's what the sword is for."

Howard kept walking, and Dante followed close behind.

"Was that what you were trying to use it for this morning? It's okay to miss your sister."

"No," Dante said. "I just wanted to make some carrots float or something dumb. I think it's the king that wants to do things like that. He talked about me doing those things for him, with him."

They were nearly at the house, the other three dogs lopping over to join Miles and Deano.

"You're smart to resist the temptation," Howard said. "I'm proud of you. You were raised well, Dante."

"Martha was raised well, too, she just made some mistakes," Dante said. "My parents are actually pretty awesome."

"I know," Howard said. "Hey, I hear James Taylor playing. That means Shanna's in a good mood. Let's see what we can get into, eh? Whaddaya say?"

Dante felt tranquil for the first time in a long time. In spite of everything, it was good to be heard. It was good to feel so welcomed and accepted, even though he couldn't help but feeling like he was messing things up left and right.

A big tree with little white flowers seemed to have grown in front of the house since they had been out. It was bountiful; Dante had no idea how he hadn't seen its beauty.

He thought Martha would have liked Casa de Shannibald.

The smell of sweet cinnamon kissed Jerrold's nose. He had never before smelt anything so good. The air in the kitchen was so rich it was buttery, like a kind of warmth was engulfing everything they touched.

Jerrold was on mixing duty, and was whipping together the drys and the wets. The sticky paste was thickening and his wrists were getting tired, but he didn't mind at all.

Shanna was lining baking sheets while Marisol shaped the first batch. Given Jerrold's appetite, they all agreed that it would be smart to make a double.

"Fire and Rain" chimed from a little speaker in the kitchen, and Shanna's stringy vibrato sang right along. Marisol hummed along, never having heard James Taylor before today, but loving the old timey pop vibes.

She asked to play some music next, and Shanna happily sang "sure."

"Hey ho," Howard said, pushing the door open. "Smells like Cinco de Mayo!"

"We don't just make pastries on Cinco de Mayo, Howie," Marisol smiled. "Whenever we want. It's not that uncommon, ya know."

"Oh I'm sorry, Marisol," Howard said, throwing an arm around her shoulder. "I'm being insensitive. It smells great is what I should have said."

"No problem," Marisol winked. "I love baking almost as much as pottery and coding."

"You should have seen this one!" Jerrold added. "When we were at that art store, she was just going to *town* on a beautiful flower!"

"Not surprised," Howard said. "You kids are all talented. I bet your parents are very proud of each of you."

"I don't know," Jerrold said. "It feels like they like the idea of me. But not who I really am. I've been thinking about that stuff a lot."

Marisol popped a sheet of conchas out of the oven. They rattled onto the burners of the oven. Each was a little pouch of delight and memory. She loaded another sheet and dropped the just-baked ones onto a bright orange Shasta plate. She set them on the kitchen table.

"Let's get this party started," Howard said. "Tiger deserves it."

As they made more conchas, Howard taught Jerrold and Dante a peanut butter and oat dog treat recipe he used for his "kids" all the time. They whipped together some of the no-bake goodness and listened to the 1970s pop music. Eventually Marisol played some banda music and Dante threw on some AC/DC. Decidedly the rock music threw off the vibe, so Jerrold played a little K-Pop later, and that just about worked.

Bottles of soda and a card table in hand, Shanna led the way to the Secret Place. The happy willow branches enshrouded them as they set up their party. Against the tree, Shanna set the table, and on top of the table Marisol set the conchas. As the swarm of dogs joined them, Howard tossed them the tiny, doughy treats. Jerrold giggled as Deano seemed to eat his hand, slobbering for his treat.

It was a beautiful celebration. Howard and Shanna told stories of Tiger, about her exploits of heroic valor, some true and some made up, and they all laughed and slapped their knees just to make sure everyone knew how funny they thought it was.

The conchas were unreal. Perfect little treats made with more than just love—made with spirit, with pride. Marisol loved how much the rest of them loved them. She thought she might bring some to school someday. If she ever went back.

She thought about how she had reached her limit, and was curious if limits couldn't be given a second chance. She jammed another concha in her mouth and came back into this moment with her friends.

They lowered Tiger's body into the plot. It was sad to see her go, but since they had such a good party, it felt more like Tiger was graduating high school and not dead. Like she was going to someplace much, much better than this place. Which was saying a lot because the Secret Place was so cool.

Chapter 17

THE BANGING OF POTS and pans woke Marisol in the morning. She jumped out of bed and rushed into the hall to see Howard walking up and down the hall in camouflage fatigues with a wooden spoon and a big cauldron.

"Wake up, wake up, wake up, wake up," Howard boomed.

She looked around the corner of the hall and saw that Dante and Jerrolds' sleeping spots were empty.

"Howard," Marisol said. He was so engrossed in his military drill she could barely be heard. "HOWARD!"

He quit marching and looked at her, a man peering out of dirty spectacles.

"Where is everyone? What are you doing?"

"Oh," he looked at his feet. "The dogs woke up the boys, so they're outside with Shanna on a walk."

"Why are you acting like it's summer camp or something?"

"I just thought it'd be a rousing way to get in the spirit of things," he said.

Marisol folded her arms, but then just laughed. Howard cracked a grin.

"Hungry, kiddo?"

"Yes, please," Marisol said.

The two of them were still in the kitchen working on eggs and bacon when Shanna came in with six dogs and the two travelers following her inside.

"Heard anything?" Howard asked Dante.

"No," Dante said. "He said he wouldn't be denied, so maybe he doesn't want to *get* denied by talking to me, since I'd just ignore him."

"Well," Howard dished up the rest of the group with their own highly caloric animal based breakfast. "We know what he wants. The sword. So let's bring the tent down on this circus freak in the most fitting way possible."

Marisol went to the guest room and brought out the artifact. The group was silent as she removed the shawl and left it on the table. It emanated the same raw power that it had in the cave.

"The garden?" Marisol asked.

"Where else?" Shanna winked.

They all walked into the patches of rhubarb and sprigs of fennel. The dogs scattered, but Miles made his way over with the group and lay down at Dante's feet.

Marisol took her stance: feet apart, heels dug in, and hands wrapped firmly around the hilt. The mold of the sword took to her just like it had before—like Marisol's hands had been the ones to shape the sword in the first place.

Air pressurized around her and the whites of her eyes painted over her irises. Diamonds seemed to glitter around the sword as the shine of the stone overcame the little clearing between the rosemary bushes.

She cleared her mind and filled it again with the image of the cave. The need to make it go away. The want to make it-

As though some invisible barrier had been suddenly struck, Marisol flew backward. The sword sailed across the yard as Marisol whipped in a circle and crashed into some watermelons.

"Oh my god," Shanna said. "Howie, things are getting out of hand."

"You know I already took care of things," Howard whispered to her. "We're in a controlled environment. That's what's important. Let me make sure she's okay."

He walked over to Marisol just as Jerrold helped her up. Dante, concerned, sat on the porch with a labradoodle named Lilly. Tiger's sister.

"What happened? Did you feel the sword?" Jerrold asked.

"I did, but just as I decided to bring down the cave it was like I had punched a window. It was like 'four-oh-four not found' kind of thing."

"What does *that* mean?" Howard said.

"Like she couldn't select that option," Jerrold said. "Do you think it has to do with that 'king' guy?"

"No doubt," Dante said. "If he's lasted this long, he's clearly super powerful. He's gotta be protecting himself."

"The sword won't work on the cave as long as that monster is inside," Howard muttered.

Howard walked back inside, muttering to himself, and Shanna mentioned how the kids might want to come back inside to relax. They were tense, though. Confidence was harder to stick on than they thought—it was like they could cycle to greatness and back to the worstness in just a day.

All three found their way into the living room and were welcomed warmly by their dog companions. Goose and Jake nuzzled Jerrold's legs, licking them like ferocious bears lapping up rare, loose honey.

"Look," Howard had a big mug of coffee in his hand. "We have to go back to work today. The Ore-gone-ian has to be a respite for weary fishies like yourself." His walrus mustache was spread in an upside down U around his smile.

"And it seems like there is nothing to be done about that cave today. That looked like it hurt, Marisol," Shanna said, wringing her hands. "You okay?"

"Eh," Marisol folded her arms. "It wasn't too bad. More of a shock, really."

Shana and Howie told them to just stay put for a few hours until one of them could come back and check in on them. They had TV, Roku, and a fridge full of boujee food. At six, if they would feed the dogs, that would be great.

Howard and Shanna took off in their trusty Subaru. The kids watched them go like an excited pooch saying farewell to its family for the day.

"I think I'll take a walk," Jerrold said. "I have some thinking to do. Sort of a 'listen to the Beatles and think a lot' type of thinking."

"Ooh," Dante said. "White people music."

"What can I say," Jerrold said. "My pigment betrays me."

"And you're 14," Dante shook his head. "A regular wordsmith."

"I'm going to watch Bill Nye," Marisol said. "And eat hummus. Feel free to join."

The woods were inviting. Like they had always been a warm space for folks like Jerrold. Jerrold took to the grounds and kept Lilly at his heel. He wanted to check his text messages and see if Toby had sent him anything. Sent *Jerrold* anything. Jerrold was figuring all that out.

Lilly walked like Tiger had died, head hanging a bit lower, eyes cast down. Jerrold didn't expect this. He had never spent much time around dogs. He didn't have animals back in Eugene. His parents would never allow it. They had far too much to worry about with just Jerrold—he thought they would go into multiple conniptions if they added even a goldfish to their 'perfect' mix.

The flag pole outside school flickered in his mind. He saw it differently now. He saw it like a beacon for the next time school ended. For the next time Jerrold might see Toby, and when all those kids might see Jerrold next.

He shuddered a little.

Lilly barked and Jerrold giggled. All of that wasn't with him now.

Dante had joined Marisol on the couch for the biggest chill session they'd each had since last Summer vacation. Bill Nye droned on about how tectonic plates shifted. They both thought there were no more appropriate episode to start with.

"This dude, Bill Nye," Dante said. "Pretty sure he lives in Washington."

"Not surprised," Marisol said between bites of carrot. "Don't all wealthy White people live in Washington?"

"That sass though! Yikes, Marisol!"

She smiled, but meant it.

"You're not wrong," Dante agreed, reaching for a few bell peppers.

The day rolled on and Jerrold listened to a few repeats of Eleanor Rigby before finding his way back to the house.

"Hey gang," Jerrold said as he walked in.

"Jerry," Dante said, his eyes never leaving the TV. "What is the what, man?"

"Eh," Jerrold said. "I'm. . .I'm hanging out. Maybe going to read some Goosebumps. What are you watching?"

"Bill Nye," Dante said. "Pretty fascinating stuff."

"Should we do something with the sword? It might want to be used," Jerrold said, gripping his hands.

Marisol thought about that for a second.

"I think it needs to rest after this morning. That's a nice way to think though, Jerrold."

He shrugged and sat down with them on the couch.

They all *had* felt that about the sword. It wasn't like the earth itself had decided to spit Brewer's Yawn back into existence—even if Bill Nye didn't know that. There was some type of life force to that pink stone. Like the sword had once been a deeper part of the formation of things.

They didn't have the answers to where the sword came from, the dark voice may not even know, but everyone from Howard to those nasty kobolds could feel the vibrancy from the sword. Talking about it didn't make any difference—what words were there for such an integrally natural thing?

Jerrold hadn't been sitting with them for more than fifteen minutes when Shanna burst into the house. She was back sooner than any of the three had assumed that she would be. Her face was even whiter than Bill Nye's.

"Slow day, Shanna?" Jerrold asked.

"If only," Shanna said. "Kids, come over here."

She sat at the table and pulled out her iPhone. She swiped it to life and held the tool high above her head, exhaling long and slow, so the kids could read *The Bulletin* article she had crossed.

"Disturbing Scene at Central Oregon Cultural Museum Proves Fatal for Longtime Curator"

Bend, OR. Updated at 12:09 p.m. A break-in at 14th Avenue and Salmon Way in Bend, Oregon, tripped the police blotter at 7:41 a.m. Curator Marjorie Helm was found on scene unconscious with numerous incisions and lacerations on her legs.

"Read the whole thing," Shanna said, her voice a rose closing at dusk.

The only exhibit interfered with at Central Oregon Cultural Museum was the Klamath and Kalapuya exhibit. Two cases full of spears and Native tools were completely destroyed, the artifacts strewn around the room in the debris.

"We assume the assailants were looking for something and didn't find it," Police Chief Butch Reynolds said.

Helm is being treated at Bend General Hospital and as of now is expected to make a full recovery.

"As of now," Jerrold said, his words tumbling from his lips to the kitchen table.

"Okay kids," Shanna said, standing up. "I think we can make a guess at what happened."

"They're looking for the sword," Marisol said. "The kobolds. This is bad."

Shanna and Marisol started brainstorming while Jerrold and Dante sat down at the table. Dante's mind flooded with all of his usual anxious thoughts—all the ones that didn't help him a bit. That's when he heard it creep into his brain again.

"A shame," the voice spoke, as velveteen as before. "My couriers were confused. A valiant attempt on their part though, don't you think?"

"Guys! He's talking to me!"

Shanna, Jerrold, and Marisol all whipped their heads toward Dante.

"Recite my words like a choir, Dante. Your choice. Bring the sword *back* to my prison. Release me. My next envoy won't be so courteous," the voice spoke. "And please don't mistake my generosity for weakness."

Dante did exactly what the king said: he wrote the message down on a pad of paper that Shanna foisted his way. On the lined yellow paper, he wrote out the entire thing.

Howard came home just as dark began to swallow Casa de Shannibald. They told him what had happened at the museum, how the voice had called to Dante yet again.

"Oofdah," Howard slapped his palms on the table. He leaned back in his chair.

"I don't know what else to say, kids. We either wait for this freakazoid to hurt someone else, or we go back into that cave."

"You two shouldn't come," Marisol said. "I don't think it would work."

"What do you mean?" Shanna said. "You can't go in there by yourselves."

"We already did," Marisol said, her voice a firm arrow. "And I mean that he's not going to *let* you back in. Why else is he only talking to Dante? Why else could we not just close the cave from here?"

All five of them sat like stunned audience members, as quiet and orderly as they could stand.

"Well we better put fresh batteries in our head lamps," Jerrold said. "As much as I love spelunking, doing it in the dark is just *not* Triple A safety approved."

Dante chuckled quietly, and Howard smiled beneath his big white mustache.

"Let's sleep on it," Shanna said. "If no one has to go back, no one goes back. We're lucky to have gotten all three of you out as it is. And to have that sword."

Marisol looked toward her room. She felt the throbbing of the sword, its energy residing just on the other side of these few walls.

"You're right that we should count our blessings," Marisol said. "But I'm not so sure."

Jerrold and Dante set up their bedding on the couch and air mattress, and Marisol went to her guest bed. The house felt sullen, like the precipice of war had somehow fallen over the building.

Chapter 18

MARISOL, DANTE, AND JERROLD made the decision the next morning to go down to the museum. It wasn't that they *wanted* to, but it seemed like the *only* thing to do. Or so Shanna had suggested. They left the sword at home. Nothing about the kobold attack downtown screamed that they should bring the artifact any closer to the little beasts than need be.

The place was really a mess. The street was sectioned off with noisy orange cones. There were more cops than when they had gone into Brewer's Yawn, and there were even more reporters. A funny cave was less interesting than a vandal breaking and entering into the local educational center. If it bleeds, it reads.

"What you kids doin' here?" an old White cop asked them. He was about as stereotypical as it gets—he even sported a jelly filled donut in his free hand. The other was busy holding a mug of coffee.

"We wanted to visit the museum," Marisol said. She barely held eye contact with the overweight official.

"Not a good day," he replied. "If you couldn't tell. You can't be disturbing evidence."

"But isn't it open? We looked it up on Google and it said so," Jerrold said.

"You can't go in today," the officer said.

"We're open, ya know," a voice loosed from inside.

The officer rolled his eyes and sighed. Then he stopped mid-bite.

"Heck, you can go inside," he said. His shoulders slumped and his body seemed to exhale. Then he turned and lumbered away.

"He must be more interested in donut and coffee consumption than protection," Jerrold shrugged.

The three travelers walked to the front of the store. It was less glass-filled than they expected. There had been a concerted effort to sweep, it seemed. Whatever riotous event had transpired the day before was already becoming a foggy memory.

The door was open, and the orange sign read "OPEN" in old-timey block letters. It seemed like the whole front of the Central Oregon Cultural Museum was dropped out of a Western movie, some kind of cowboy adventure where the stores all looked like 2-D props.

The three kids looked at each other before Marisol took the first step forward. She was getting a lot better at that part. Dante and Jerrold followed her into the ruinous building.

Strewn along the glass-coated carpet, the kids saw four clear and colorful snack bar wrappers. Dark chocolate cherry, apple cinnamon, oats and almonds, fruits and nuts; it was like a library of flavors laying at their feet.

Through their gaze they saw a fifth wrapper falling to the ground—pecan blueberry.

"They're pretty good," the same voice said. "And healthy, and whatnot. Only five grams of sugar."

They looked up to the counter and saw a sharp featured, leathery man. His eyes were thin and heavy, like a tired hound. Even at first sight, there was every reason to believe that he had been born in this museum, and that he would die there.

"That's great," Marisol looked at his dusty but sterling name plate. "Benjamin."

"Mr. Benjamin Kamkoff to you, girlie," the man said, grinning.

"Your name plate only says Benjamin," Marisol said, folding her arms.

Benjamin stood up and cleared his throat. The gravely movement of bits of nuts and oats struck the silence of the room.

"What business have you got at the Cultural Center today?"

"We wanted to see the artifacts section," Marisol said. "And try and learn about what happened."

"Some kind of Scooby-Doo stuff, huh?" Benjamin asked.

"Yeah!" Jerrold said.

"Not now, Jerry," Dante said.

Benjamin got up and walked away from the counter. He flipped his hand over his shoulder, gesturing for the kids to follow him. They followed him as he trundled along a narrow hallway, antique store style stacks of photos and letters ascending on either side.

Along the carpet there were dirty foot prints, the prints being no bigger than a rabbit's foot. Two tracks lined the hall, and just near each print there were scratches and dents on the cases nearby.

"Poor Mrs. Helm. She'll be alright, but she took a fall for true."

When they got to the rear of the museum, they saw a few steps descending into a wide rectangular room. The walls were lined with glass cases displaying masks and spears. One of the tallest cases was shattered, and there was police tape plastered like a hurricane's wreckage.

"The little rascals did the deed back here," Benjamin muttered.

"Which little rascals? Do you know who did it?" Dante asked. Jerrold and Marisol were confused, too.

Benjamin turned his head aside and began to rifle through some of the nearby post cards. They were ancient things, things turned yellow by time and forgetfulness. Like a heavy fog had descended down upon them, Benjamin began to speak:

"There was an energy, a power, that the Earth had given to the people of this land. It created a home for that power—a vehicle. It took the shape and size of a sword. This is not native to this land; the Earth wanted the people here to be bewildered. The power had a life of its own."

Marisol, Dante, and Jerrold watched the man as he sat down on the steps. His body sagged with tiredness. His face spoke more than his words.

"It's been such a long time," Benjamin went on. "No one in my corner of the world would have thought that it'd come back. But it must've been inside that blasted cave again."

"Are you talking about the sword?" Dante asked.

"Yeah," Benjamin said. "Yeah I s'pose I am. You kids know about it. I knew you knew about it the second you walked up to the dang counter."

"How!?" Jerrold asked.

"Why else would you come in here the day after the break in asking about the artifacts section? We haven't *got* an artifacts section. Just means you were looking for something specific."

"Oh," Jerrold said. "Good point."

"We're sorry," Marisol said.

"For what? Have you *got* the thing? Or just sorry for my people in general? Like everyone is?"

They didn't know what to say. Benjamin stood up and walked to the big shattered case. It had a great map of the area painted on the rear of the box, detailing where each tribe resided and still resides. He pointed to a part of the map, near the bottom, that detailed a few stories. One square had a picture of a sword, a rough drawing, with a big fat jewel in the blade.

"There's all kinds of legends," Benjamin said. He unwrapped another snack bar. "Some true. Some not. People from all over the world have their own legends. It's crucial to understand something."

They looked at Benjamin. He swallowed a big bite of snack bar.

"Legends have minds of their own. They want what they want. That goes for the good ones *and* the bad ones."

None of them had anything to say. Tell him about the sword? He didn't even seem trustworthy at this point. He could be working with Karrabad for all they knew, or influenced by his powers in the same way that Dante had experienced. He led them to the front of the store again.

"It's alright," Benjamin said. "You kids don't need to worry about whatever you do or don't know about these old tales. It's just a hard time to be a Native is all."

"I understand," Marisol said.

Benjamin squinted his eyes again.

"Maybe you do. Well in any-"

A clanging outside interrupted their conversation. Jerrold dashed out the front door as Benjamin whipped around the desk, seeming to jump over it in his rush. In the street there were no more cops or reporters, somehow all seemed to have gone away at the same time.

Two kobolds were banging against the wall of the old building. They wore rags like lost children. It was like they thought their tiny fists and tools could crack the concrete. Their eyes were red like little, ripe strawberries.

"They're back," Benjamin said.

He rolled up the sleeves of his checkered flannel. Dante, Jerrold, and Marisol all joined him as they marched toward the two tiny warriors, each of the three as scared as could be, but the kobolds stopped in mid-motion. They swiveled like marionettes toward the four museum-goers. Each opened their mouths like bullhorns, and with unmoving lips a voice issued forth:

"I'll have the sword yet. Return it to the cave or I will send an army of these degenerates to bring doom upon this town. I've sent but three so far. Imagine three hundred. . .or three thousand."

The two kobolds clamped their mouths like robots and, like lifeless bodies hit by lightning, they jumped back to action and quickly scurried away.

Benjamin sighed and scratched his head through his long black hair. Slowly, from the sides of their eyes, they saw police officers and reporters fading into view. As though a cloud had risen from the pavement and revealed the true world again.

"You kids had better get home," Benjamin said. "Or wherever you're staying now."

"How can we help?" Marisol asked.

"Just keep on doing whatever you *can* do," he said. "But don't get too ahead of yourselves. Even an elephant gets eaten one bite at a time."

They took a Lyft back to Casa de Shannibald. It beat bussing around, but the little dents of money were wearing them thin. It wasn't great that each driver seemed more confused and bitter than the last.

"If it wasn't for this PC bullpuckey we'd have had a president like this *years* ago," their driver steamed.

"I'm sorry, but how did we get on this topic?" Dante asked, rolling his eyes.

"We're *always* on this topic in *my* car," the old timer steamed.

"Good to know," Dante said as he readied a one-star review.

The three got out of the car and walked down the winding dirt path. They said nothing to each other, a sticky silence hanging between them like the sugary pull of those snack bars Benjamin devoured.

It was late enough for Howard and Shanna to both be home—they had a college kid come in to close the place up on Sundays. The Ore-Gone-Ian shuttered for the day, they sat in the kitchen and drank tea as the kids knocked the day's debris off of their shoes.

"How'd the museum look?" Howard asked. Little driblets of tea soaked in his epic mustache.

"Bad," Jerrold said. "But that guy who worked there knew a lot about the sword."

"Really?" Shanna said. "I didn't know any guys worked there at all. I swore it was Mrs. Helm and two young women from the college who interned there. Are you sure he *worked* there?"

"Think so. He was really intense," Dante said. "And he really liked snack bars."

"And two kobolds showed up while we were there," Marisol said.

"Oh my word," Shanna said. "That's no good at all. Alright, tell us what happened."

The three fishies relayed their most recent encounter with the king's minions. They explained how Benjamin thought the agents of the cave, both the sword and Karrabad, had their own agenda. Howard and Shanna tapped their teas with their fingers—it was pretty cute. They both *hrm*ed in the same way, wondering out loud. Each of the kids smiled a bit as they watched their hosts partner-think.

"I hate to say it," Shanna said. "But it does seem like someone will have to go back into that cave."

"Shanna's right," Howard said. "And, Marisol, you were saying you didn't think she or I could join you. Why's that again?"

Marisol thought about the sword, and she thought about King Karrabad. She remembered the way that it seemed like she had hit some enormous invisible wall when she tried to collapse the cave before.

"I don't think they'd let you in," she said.

"They who?" Howard asked.

"The kobold king. *Or the sword.*"

"Fascinating," Howard twirled his mustache. "How do you figure?"

"I think they have been planning these things more than we realize," she said. "Jerrold's vision in the cave could have been the sword giving us the tools to find it. All the police and reporters disappearing at the right times. This kind of stuff. Who knows if the cave would even *be* there if you two tried to come with."

"Like the sword wants to be free," Jerrold said.

"And like King Karrabad wants to be free, too," Dante said.

All five sat in the kitchen as Miles and Jake lay at their feet. The dogs' eyes drooped more than before, and their bodies sagged. They were short one of their cadre, and they clearly felt the loss.

"So that's it then," Howard said. "You'd better not waste any time."

Marisol nodded, and Jerrold produced a comically loud gulp. Dante just smiled and shook his head. They walked to the back of the house and packed their bags while Howard and Shanna packed up batteries and cookies. As she tucked the sword inside her backpack, zipping it to the blade on both sides, Marisol came upon the little doll she had been given on the bus and made sure to tuck it into the side of her backpack, its presence somehow emboldening her. Jerrold grabbed his lacrosse stick. Dante made sure to wear his running shoes.

Howard loaded all their bags in the back of the Subaru. The dogs barked their goodbyes, hopping on the car and on each other in their excitement. John Denver played softly in the car. Shanna waved goodbye from the porch like a widow on her watch to the expanse of the sea.

"You've got your batteries?" Howard asked.

"Yeah," they replied.

"And extra clothes?"

"No," they replied.

"Okay, that's fair. What about snacks?"

"Howard," Marisol said. "We're fine. We've been in before."

"I know, but I didn't know you kids like this last time. I'm worried about you already."

"No need to fear, Jerry Seinfeld is here!" Jerrold called out.

Howard looked at him in the rearview mirror. The four of them had only known each other four days. In this moment, that didn't really matter.

"I'll expect you all back tomorrow evening," he said.

"Understood, Howie," Dante said.

The car zoomed along the lonely rural roads. Only a few other cars passed them as they drove. The time for talking was through. The time for thinking was all that remained.

Chapter 19

THE TRIO ARRIVED AT dusk, the warm Oregon sun turning now into moonlight. Only two cop cars were spotted in the woods at all, and neither seemed too interested in the cave.

It was the same cave as before, and it was as bright as they had left it. Marisol's powers had staying power, and, from how Dante heard it, that's exactly what bothered King Karrabad the most.

"We must be the ones that woke him up," Jerrold said, as quiet as a kobold, so not very quiet at all.

"We'll be the ones to put him back to sleep, too," Dante said, sounding as brave as he could muster.

"If he wasn't down that crawl space when we came in the first time. . .I wonder how we find him," Marisol said.

They stood in the alcove and thought.

"Hey," Dante said. "We know we can't use the sword's power on the outside of the cave. But what about the inside, like with the lights?"

Jerrold looked a little confused. Marisol's eyes crinkled up in thought as her head nodded slowly up and down.

Dante continued, "I mean, if it can make a play ground pop up out of the ground, then it should be able to find this dude, right?"

Marisol gripped the sword again and felt the power swell inside of her, all around her. A wall of earth in the corner of the room, along the left side beyond the crawl space, grew a line in its face. The line heaved and ho'd and spread itself into a bar, and then into a gap. This eventual divide split the wall in two, making a gap about three Jerrolds wide.

Faster each time, Marisol made what she needed, and the power began to recede. She stowed the sword, nodded to her two compadres, and the three began walking down the new path. It was a barren way, with none of the familiar –ites and –mites. On account of its newness perhaps, there was no light inside the corridor. The three fishies remained quiet as they moved deeper into the darkness.

Light opened in front of them at some point. Marisol's reshaping of the cave affected all of those pockets, even the ones that they had not seen. What they saw now was remarkable.

A larger than possible room opened before them. A few dark passageways lined the walls like tracks in a video game, and a veritable bounty of stalagmites and stalactites sprouted up like a railway spike graveyard.

At the rear of the giant space they saw thick coils of rock stretching across the back wall like some elaborate stone art project. There was some huge feature in the middle, like a nervous system with a tumor.

King Karrabad was where the brain of each kobold went to die. He was in the back of the cave, his body wrapped in earthen coils. His body was barely anything—a tiny, flimsy puppet's frame. But his head was a pulsing, grotesque globe. Little whiskers and hairs dotted around his snout and mouth, a cartoonishly exaggerated version of his children, and great pustules and warts splayed like mines across the field of his face. Both of his swollen dark red eyes resembled pools of hot paint.

"Dante," it spoke, though its mouth never moved. "You came."

They heard his voice inside their minds, and they saw the top of the creature's head pulse and quiver like gelatin. It had an unmoving expression of smirk and rage.

"Not to help you escape," Dante said. "To make sure you *never* do. Hate has no place in our world. Or it has too much a place already without you trying to make it any worse."

"I know you didn't come to liberate me from my prison," King Karrabad spoke. "I've been following you. With the same power that the small one uses to see the truth of things."

"Ew," Jerrold said.

"I knew you would refuse my offer of power," the king went on. "Though I had hope you might change your mind. It could only be you, Dante."

"I don't like that," Dante said. "It's like you're saying I'm the only one stupid or weak enough to fall for your tricks. That only makes me happier to do what we came to do, Karrabad."

"You came to hurt me, Dante," it said softly. "But you're starting to understand where I'm coming from. In a way, we are starting to become friends."

From the rear of the cave, swarms of kobolds came frenzying forward as before. Somehow this time there were even more. They carried their spears and picks, chanting their angry slurs. Marisol readied the sword.

"No, Marisol," Dante said, putting his hand on her shoulder. "Remember what we learned. The King feeds on that power. And we can't use it to unmake him any ways. We have to use the sword against him."

"Then how are we going to stop the freaky small ones!?" Jerrold chimed in.

"We'll figure it out."

Marisol thrust the sword into Dante's arms, their eyes meeting.

"Here's your chance to practice, Dante. Good luck."

She grabbed Jerrold's arm and the two of them ran toward the kobolds. Dante about-faced and stared at King Karrabad. Then he ran, too.

Chapter 20

JERROLD AND MARISOL RAN headlong at the cavalcade of cave dwelling monsters. Marisol felt impassioned, like Pancho Villa. Jerrold was scared stiff, like Scooby-Doo. But fear or not, they both ran toward the shambling mass.

Marisol just saw os and 1s, suppressing her fear and turning it into a problem to solve, just like she'd always done.

"Let's lead them off to the left," Marisol said. "This is just another puzzle."

"You're so optimistic about this stuff, Marisol," Jerrold said. "I, on the other hand, am frickin' petrified."

"See those puddles?" Marisol pointed as they started to near the army. "This cave is wet. Like damp."

"Following you so far," Jerrold said.

They neared the head of the legion and then pivoted to the left. The host followed them, their chittering weapons safely diverted from Dante.

"That means the stalactites and stalagmites, or *which*ever, are loose," Marisol said.

"Is that how that works?" Jerrold said.

"I think so," Marisol said. "It's like making pottery. It should be more shapeable."

"So," Jerrold picked up his heels as one kobold got close to his sneakers with its tiny pitchfork.

"So pick up the speed and do as I do, chico," Marisol said.

They both sped down a long corridor that led away from their entrance tunnel, and away from the big room that held the king.

Unsurprising to either of them, the path was windy and mystifying, seeming like a maze lifted off the back of a highway diner's kid's menu. Rough calling and chanting came from behind them. Through the maze they went.

"I'll stand behind this one, and you behind that one. Be quiet so they don't notice you," Marisol said.

"Okay. . ." Jerrold did as he was told. He saw Marisol plant her feet and place her hands against the rocky spike, and he mimicked.

The army of mini troglodytes found them at last. Their haplessness didn't detract from their scariness, thought Jerrold, or from their poky weapons.

They went right in front of him. Not a one had the brains to notice him at all. Once the deep throng of assailants safely passed by Jerrold, Marisol took it upon herself to start rocking her stalagmite loose. Jerrold made sure to do the same.

The kobolds splashed through shallow puddles and could hardly hear the noise. By the time they did realize what was happening, it was way too late.

Marisol's stalagmite crashed down in front of the kobolds, even squishing a few of the little leaders, and Jerrold's did the same to the rear. The kobolds were too small and too short-sighted to notice that they had been trapped; they clawed and bit at the rocks, but they couldn't free themselves from the pen that had been dropped around them.

"Good thinking, Marisol!"

"Thanks Jerry," Marisol said, stepping over her stalagmite and skirting along the side of the kobolds. "I just thought about that running of the bulls thing?"

"Isn't that a Mexican thing?"

"No, but it's pretty cool. It should keep them trapped long enough for us to get out of here."

They flipped toward their compadre, and ran.

King Karrabad's eyes, devoid of pupils though they were, still followed Dante as he began to encircle the underground lord. Dante wasn't sure why he was hesitant to strike—it should be easy. Just walk up and *slice*.

Dante came just a few feet away from the enormous monstrosity. Its head was so big, eyes so far apart, that it couldn't make eye contact with Dante while he was this close. The king's mouth, just below Dante's waist, gently gnashed and crashed, its devastating but now useless teeth a flair.

He plunged the sword forward. As he did so, he felt his body freeze in the middle of the strike, his muscles reverbing against themselves. It was like someone hit pause on his life. He was even suspended in mid-air.

"Enough time to train the mind gives one abilities beyond the realm of imagination, Dante," the king said, his voice an even tone. "You'll never be able to strike me."

"Is that right?" Dante thought. He tried to think of the next move. He tried to figure out the puzzle, like Marisol. He tried to think of something witty to say, some dazzling trick, like Jerrold.

"It's a futile effort, but I'm glad you're making it. With the sword so close, and your friends only momentarily stopping my children, it won't be long until I use its crystalline power to free myself from this ageless penitentiary."

"Your beautiful big head can't free you all on its own, huh?" Dante asked, his body still mid-attack.

"It can. It brought you here. Your spirit."

"You can't handle my spirit," Dante said. His mind was churning, trying to figure out *something*.

"I can, Dante," he said. "Your mind is too weak. You're the weakest of your party. You're the useless one."

He's right. You're stupid. You're no good, and you've already messed everything up. Dante kept telling himself these stories and they just weren't helping.

"You're wrong," Dante said. "It's not all about the mind. I said my *spirit*. You can't handle my spirit."

Dante turned off his brain. He let go of trying to figure it all out, and of trying to engage with the king. He let himself be okay with not knowing, and when he did that he was finally able to begin.

The muscle fibers in his arm split from the psionic grasp molecule by molecule, reversing the polarity. Dante felt it happen, noticed himself not trying too hard. The sword swam in the barrier just a mite closer.

King Karrabad's little body fidgeted.

"What's wrong, boss? Your negative brain doesn't seem to be infecting mine anymore."

"It's a subtle fix," the king said.

In a heartbeat Dante was shunted backward to the other side of the room. The sword was still frozen, his body hardly responding.

In his mind he saw blue skies. He allowed in some birds. Martha was there.

One foot went up, then down again.

"No!" King Karrabad pushed him back another ten yards, but Dante persisted. One foot went up, then down again. His friends would have been proud to see him push through the psychic block that the monster crushed against him. Dante pushed back.

He slogged forward, back to his position above the king, his arms still frozen in the mental blockade. The rivulets of wormy brain on top of King Karrabad's head quivered and pulsed like mad as he worked feverishly to stop Dante.

"Dante, it's not too late. Lay the sword at my feet. The power would-"

"Its a futile effort," Dante said. "And honestly I'm not glad you're making it. It just makes it sadder."

He drove the tip of the scimitar into one of the enormous red eyes on the kobold lord's head. A noise like radio static blasted Dante in his mind, but he dug the sword deeper and deeper. As though he were burying King Arthur's fabled sword in the first place, Dante made sure to push the sword all the way until he hit stone.

King Karrabad's psionic voice buzzed and echoed, but faded now to a whimper. Dante sweat and panted, his skin cool and damp. Everything seemed blurry, but he steadied his breathing. The only sound was his breath, and the drip of the king's blood splashing to the floor.

Dante looked at the ruin of what he had done. It wasn't pride that he felt, but it wasn't shame either. Just a strangeness. It didn't feel like ending a life, nothing like what he had heard kids at Lincoln go through, but it didn't feel good.

"Dante!" Marisol shouted. She had outpaced Jerrold and found Dante still standing over the king's corpse.

"Whoa, Marisol," Dante asked, snapping out of all his freaked-outness. "Are you okay?"

"Yeah, we're fine," Marisol said. "You. . .did it! Wow, that was faster than I expected."

"Really? It felt like it took a lifetime."

"Yeah, that has to be hard," Marisol walked over to him. She placed a hand on his shoulder. "But you did it! You really did it."

"Did *what*? I feel like crap," Dante said. He gave Marisol back the sword.

"Saved the world," Marisol said, grinning. "Or at least rural Eastern Oregon."

Jerrold came back into the room, huffing.

"All the kobolds turned into dust! Did you. . ."

"He's gone," Marisol said. She pushed the sword back toward Dante. "He did it!"

"You did it!" Jerrold said.

"Everyone *stop* saying 'you did it.' Let's just get out of here," Dante said.

"Alright," Jerrold said. "But it is pretty cool. How you did it."

"Ugh," Dante marched forward, smiling just a bit.

That's when the radio silence reared to life again. It became so loud that Dante, Marisol, and Jerrold fell to their knees, yelling.

King Karrabad's body wriggled a bit, and the head produced a sort of heaving sound. The cave began to shake again.

"You should not have upset me, Dante," the voice hummed. "And you should not have aimed for my eye."

The rocky chains tightened again and pulled Karrabad toward the wall, cementing him once again in his familiar place. The kobold tyrant's huge head bobbled for a moment, and Dante could see a rodent like mouth open and close, blood oozing from the corners.

"I will need time to heal," the king spoke into their minds, the radio silence fading. "But I will have that. The time has come for something a bit more dramatic than I had originally seen."

Dozens of kobolds came from the walls, like they had been there all along. The armies approached the three and pinned them in the middle of the room, packing them tight against one another.

"I hope you fare well in my home. I didn't much like it there, but I couldn't make it all the way to the surface. This time will be different."

One kobold leapt toward Dante and swiped the sword.

"Damn!"

"Good bye, children," the king spoke.

A hole opened in the floor below them, and they began to plummet into a darkness unlike any they had seen before.

Chapter 21

FALLING TAKES MORE TIME than is reported. It's not the sky diving that one might imagine. Or that's what the three spelunkers were thinking as air rushed past their faces. It felt like they had been falling for weeks.

A huge pile two stories high of something caught them. Each socketed into the pile like bullets in a hay bale. When they finally scrambled their way out, they noticed the pile was made of rotten food and tattered clothes. Dante gagged. Marisol brushed herself off furiously. Jerrold actually *did* throw up.

They heard a rushing of water and looked around. If they had thought Brewer's Yawn was underground before, they just hadn't been down far enough yet. Everything was a dark gray and black, like the floors and ceilings were made of mildewed plaster. Exposed dirt bled through in patches.

An enormous water fall roared behind them. It seemed to come from nowhere, the water falling into an enormous pool. The pool was full of big bones tumbling across the surface, so that it looked like someone was cooking a stew with the water faucet running.

"Are those. . .?" Jerrold asked, his hand pointing to the far side of the garbage pile.

Little brown houses, about the size of rich people's dog houses, were stacked on top of each other like adobe homes in the canyons of New Mexico. Lights flickered dimly inside them, and chittering noises could be heard. The sound was like a swarm of cicada tap dancing.

Off to their left was a long rickety bridge, spanning a great, dark ravine, leading to another island of dark stone and little houses. It went on that like that as far as they could see.

"Move," someone said.

Marisol wheeled in a one-eighty to find the voice, but she already had a hunch to look down. There was a kobold, sporting a burlap sack-looking dress, looking up at Marisol, tapping its foot. It scratched its scales.

"Move! Quit hogging the pile!"

Marisol moved to the left, and the little critter walked headlong into the big heap of rubbish. It exited the other side carrying a few apple cores and a new burlap sack.

"Dios mio," Marisol said. "This is where they *live*. I didn't know they could talk."

"I'm gonna be sick," Jerrold said. "Again. Sorry."

"It's fine, Jerry," Dante said. "I can't believe I didn't kill him. I thought I *did* it."

They looked at Dante.

"Nobody say anything about who did or didn't do it," he said. "What do we do next?"

"We've got to find a way out," Marisol said, folding her arms. "Without the sword, we'll just have to find the way that they use to get out."

Jerrold looked to the bridge and shrugged. He started walking, the other two following. It was dilapidated enough, so they had their concerns pressing down on such a flimsy thing, but they had to admire kobold engineering—it held up.

On the next island they found slightly more infrastructure: a torch, a poorly written sign written in a language they couldn't hope to understand, and more homes. They took the next bridge. On the next island, it was more of the same, with just a bit more infrastructure. So they took the next bridge.

After following bridge after bridge, and receiving countless pallid stares from the earth dwelling kobolds, they started to hear a rhythm. A heartbeat coming from a few islands away.

"Let me stop for one second," Dante said. "I got a few snack bars to work on. Failing to kill a king takes it out of a guy."

"Hey, take it easy on yourself, you did your best," Jerrold said.

"I know, I'm just upset," Dante said. "Want one? Cranberry Apple, completely rot-free."

"You could do stand up, Dante," Jerold said.

"You know it, Jerry."

They sat on some stones near the next bridge. One of the nearby houses chittered louder than the rest, then its thatched front door swung open. A mustachioed kobold wearing a newsboy cap walked out. He stood in front of Marisol, who was sitting with her hands cupping her chin.

"'Ey," the kobold said. "Wot are ya doin' eer?"

"Why should we talk to you?" Marisol asked.

"Ay ay, I'm just a simple kobold 'ere. Me wife asks me come talk to ya, says ya sound lost, says I oughta be a good naybur, since we kobolds get a bad repatation for nayburliness, I says it don't mattah 'a *me* if I'm a good naybur. . ."

"Alright, alright," Dante says. "We're trying to find a way up."

"Up? Oh rocks they want *up* oh jeeze. That's not me speciality no no, maybe Martha but she's back inside," the kobold wrung his hands.

"Martha? Your wife's name is Martha?" Dante stands.

"That's right, married fiteen years we been," the kobold says.

"Small world. Or underworld," Dante smiles. "My name's Dante."

"I'm Jerrold!"

"I'm Marisol."

"Name's Eebee. Let's see wot Martha thinks 'bout all this."

The kobold scampers back to his hut. The door swings shut softly, and the chittering ramps up again. He returned to his 'nayburs' in no time at all.

"She's got a 'eadache. Nasty business that, but she says ya outta look for Coyote. If you keep on keepin' to these bridges, in just three more you'll get to town. E's bound to be there somewheres."

"Alright," Dante says. "Thanks, Eebee. Can we ask you what this place is called?"

"Ayyyyy don't think of it, jus' bein' a good naybur I am. We'll hope to see ya around our home someday again, that's right."

The little figure turned back around. Then back around again.

"Oh dat's roight, the name. We call this place the Neverearth. It was never supposed to be under *this* earth, but 'ere it is. 'Ows that work for yeh?"

"Um," Dante said. "I guess just fine, Eebee."

The little fellow nodded and flipped toward his little house. When he opened the door, a warm glow could be seen from the front room—it was actually pretty inviting.

Confused as they could be about just how these creatures live and behave, they marched forward along the third to last bridge. The rest of Neverearth lay directly before them.

Chapter 22

VERITABLE SKYSCRAPERS CAME INTO view. That is to say that buildings taller than any of the ones they had seen so far were popping up, but they were still made of twigs and mud.

The rhythm persisted, and they could tell what it was now: the sound of a city. It was like they had fallen into the suburbs, and were finally walking into the nightlife.

They came upon their first "street" which was like a path of stone lined by torches. Larger houses were on either side of them, some sporting quite large doors.

Marisol for one couldn't imagine what they would need doors higher than a bar stool for, but that was before she saw the boqs.

Scattered amongst the kobolds they saw men taller than any human could grow. Covered in hair, with big underbites, these people looked like they belonged in the trees, not in caves.

More and more urban-looking kobolds walked around them, and the stares were ramping up in frequency. One couple crossed the street as they walked by, and another scoffed.

"Not very friendly," Jerrold whispered. "I already miss Eebee."

"Let's just find 'Coyote' and get out of here," Dante said.

"I'm not seeing anything with the word 'Coyote' on it, are you?" Jerrold asked.

Marisol stopped and pointed.

"There it is. It says 'Coyote.'"

In a plaza where the buildings were higher than anywhere else, more like garden sheds, in the corner, was a sign. It was sandwich board style, like it could have been Bend, and it read "Coyote's." The three looked at each other incredulously.

They walked to the door and were preparing to knock when a group of kobolds, laughing and patting each other on the back, walked ahead of them, opening the door wide. Dante stuck his hand out. Marisol and Jerrold went in first.

A wall of sound hit them like a prizefighter. Kobolds and Boqs of all colors and dispositions sat at big wooden tables. The building was so large it seemed like an illusion, with a full bar and a stage. Tankards clanged and crashed, all to the tune of a kobold band that played a roguish tune. Candles and lanterns lined the walls; it felt like someone had lowered warm dimmer lights over the whole scene.

"This is like Star Wars Episode Four!" Jerrold said.

"Take it easy, Jerry," Dante said. "We're the odd ones down here. Let's not make it any more obvious."

Marisol walked toward the bar. She thought about being at school, and how she always felt like a stranger there any ways. In so many ways, this was no different.

The bar was just as densely populated, but they found three empty seats. Jerrold was fidgeting his hands, flicking his eyes back and forth. Marisol and Dante were calm.

"How are you both so relaxed?"

"I feel like a stranger at my school all the time," Marisol said. "I can't trust anyone there. Kind a familiar, actually."

Dante flipped the menu around and around, having no luck making out the chicken scratch, or in this case, kobold scratch. He passed it to Marisol.

"Yeah, I've spent so much time in stranger's homes doing stupid stuff that this doesn't feel too different for me, either," he said.

Jerrold just thought about that, tried to take it all in. Getting old sure is weird, he thought, but he also had a moment to reflect on how he lived. How the people in Eugene never did anything like this—how people like him could never relate to Marisol and Dante's experiences.

"Hungry? Or thirsty? Or a bit of both?"

The bartender was a dog, and not in a cheeky way. He was literally a dog. But also a man. He was so tall, at least seven feet, and stood on two legs. He wore a simple white blouse and brown pants. Smoky orange fur was burnt all over his body, and he had the head of a true animal.

"Hungry," Marisol said. "And we don't drink alcohol."

"I've got something up your alley, girlie," he said, winking.

He turned his back to them, and the three looked at each other with wide eyes. The music strummed on, a jazzy sound, and more and more people came into the bar. They were feeling a little claustrophobic, strangers rowdily cheering on each side of them, pressed together like a gathering of best friends.

A rosemary and sage scented salmon slapped down on the bar behind them. The bartender slid a plate of fry bread over, then crashed down three brown and steaming mugs. A few kobolds at the bar whooped and hollered:

"Smells good, boss!"

The dog man winked and smiled a long, chainsaw smile. He placed silverware down for the group, then propped his elbows on the bar.

"Something from my people. Enjoy."

Jerrold looked at the drink and pushed it a little further away, his gag reflux acting up. Marisol took the silverware and sliced a big piece of fish for herself. The taste was otherworldly—like no mercury, no toxins, and no sadness had ever entered the fish's body. Like it was from a thousand years ago, but fresher than ever. Dante tried the fry bread and was whisked away, too. They had never had food even *close* to this before.

"I think I know," Marisol said between mouthfuls. "But what is your name?"

"Folks call me Coyote, or Talapus, or even Coyotl, if you venture far enough South," the beast man said.

Jerrold slapped his hands on the table in astonishment. In the noisy bar, no one even noticed.

"We're looking for you, funny enough" Marisol said, cooler than anything.

"Oh is that so? Well I'm always in the exact same spot. This is my jail cell."

"This is your jail cell?" Dante asked.

"In a way," Coyote smiled. "Why do you care?"

"We got sent down here," Dante asked. "Wherever here is, by King Karrabad."

"Ah, Karrabad. I'm the one that trapped that grumpy old thing," Coyote's smile turned into a grin. "My people and I. My brother was too busy further West, but I saw what he was doing. That bloated rat was trying to overrun our world with his enslaved kobolds."

"Is *that* why they're so friendly down here? Because they're not enslaved?"

"Bingo, kiddo. They're just regular folks down here. From far away, sort of colonizers, but they're the ones who helped name the element cobalt. So who can blame the little crafts folk. They've been around a few centuries. Until Karrabad woke up, it was fine, but now he just hauls them up as he needs 'em. They don't much appreciate that, if you know what I mean."

Dante swirled his drink. It was some type of grotto-y thing, the kind of drink an eight-year-old makes with dirt and earthworms. Marisol ate the fry bread, too, while Jerrold was working diligently on the salmon.

"It's not great when people come into your land and start making trouble," Marisol said.

"You are preaching to the anthropomorphic choir, girlie," Coyote said. "So what are you three going to do now?"

Jerrold couldn't take it any longer.

"We need your help! To escape!"

"Ahhh, to escape," Coyote said. "Why would you *ever* want to leave? Isn't the mildew charming?"

Marisol took the last bite of salmon, wiping the plate clean, using the fry bread like it was tortilla.

"We need to go home," Marisol said. "We have to make a difference. And we have to stop King Karrabad!"

Coyote looked around the room, then tapped the shoulder of one of the Boqs. The big wild man walked behind the counter, and Coyote motioned for the three travelers to do the same. They followed him into a room in the back.

It was dark with only one lantern illuminating the space. It was a simple store room, a pantry, but there was a table in the middle.

They all sat down. It felt like an interrogation. In his own cheeky manner, Coyote lit up a cigar to set the mood.

"I want to help you," he said. "I want to want to do that. I really do. But then again, I kind a don't."

"Why?" Marisol asked.

"When I trapped King Karrabad here, when my people and I spoke with the earth to bind the invader in stone, he stole something of mine," Coyote said. "Something pretty precious."

"What was it?" Jerrold asked.

"My friend's freedom," Coyote said. "Amhuluk. He's a pal. Karrabad sent his stooges to Wapato Lake to kidnap him from his lake, and trapped him in that scary looking pool beneath the waterfall."

"Oh no!" Jerrold said. "And you're staying to keep him company?"

"Um, yeah," Coyote said. "Sure. So I need you to break him free. It should be easy for a cadre of cracker jack kids like you three."

Chapter 23

THEY LEFT COYOTE'S FEELING no better than when arrived. Another daunting challenge, not a solution. Walking back past Eebee's, they saw that the lights had gone out, so they didn't even have one last friendly face before getting back to the garbage heap.

The pool roiled as though there was a strong current running, but now they knew that it was no current. It was just Amhuluk. Coyote hadn't said what kind of guy Amhuluk was, or if he was a guy, or anything. It dawned on them that they really weren't sure how to proceed.

So Marisol took the first step. On the other side of the rotting waste there was a descending path, much like the path above the labyrinth when they first found the sword. They walked down and saw that it led down to the pool's edge.

Dinosaur-size bones floated in the mire. The tiny lake was really not so tiny—it was a lot bigger when they stood along its coast. The water was a dingy green, but where the waterfall hit the pool it appeared pristine. The smell of sulfur was strong in the air.

"Let's try walking over there," Marisol pointed to where the water crashed down.

They crept along the bank. Marisol pulled her backpack tight, and she felt the muñeca in one of her side pouches. She grabbed it and turned it over. Its presence had become a source of security for her in the short time that she had had it.

The water smelt better here. In front of them they saw a tall pillar. It looked like the type of thing a dog would be tied to in a dusty patch of yard.

But it was tall, and thick. Two heavy chains looped along the top of the post, then sagged along and across the granite floor, dipping down into the water.

Dante kicked one of the chains, regretting it as soon as he did. It was heavy like the anchor chain of a large ship. They heard a swirling in the water like a geyser was erupting.

Two dark points emerged from the surface. They grew to be five or six feet tall before they began to curve toward each other. Then another form emerged—a slimy and scaly head crested from between the two points. It was the head of something make believe, or something super old.

His head was sharp like a barracuda's, like he could have been from tropical waters. A round ring looped around his neck, and as he continued to rise the chains on the bank began to tighten. A flotilla body emerged at the base of his long, giraffe's neck. It was as black and shiny as his head.

It was his eyes that were frightening. Coyote had the eyes of a trickster, but Amhuluk had the eyes of an executioner.

"Few come this close to my pool," Amhuluk said. His voice was the deep, throaty growl of a bear. "What inspires you three?"

Dante stepped forward. Marisol clutched her muñeca, and Jerrold did his best not to faint.

"Coyote told us to set you free," Dante said. "So that you could escape!"

Amhuluk's eyes jumped between the three of them, discerning the situation. A tiny smile curled on his long, dinosaur lips.

"Eat the sky one time," Amhuluk said. "And you never hear the end of it. Trapped here. Yes, I've been so upset. *Drowning* in my sorrow. Please, come a little closer so I can tell you my tale."

Marisol noticed something odd as Amhuluk spoke. The chains attached to the pole were going slack again, totally detached from how the serpent was moving. Jerrold looked closer—the ring around Amhuluk's neck didn't have a chain attached to it at all.

"Three children did visit me once," Amhuluk said. "Who amongst you is oldest?"

"I'm eighteen," Dante said.

Amhuluk struck his eyes upon Dante. Then Dante took the initiative and walked forward. Marisol put out a hand to try and stop him but it was too late. Amhuluk brought his head down in a crushing arc, and his horns caught Dante and Jerrold in their wake. He threw them into the pool.

"Dios mio!"

Amhuluk laughed a staccato, bass laugh.

"A good bit of fun," Amhuluk said. "I was worried I would only ever be drowning things attached to that boring pole."

Jerrold surfaced quickly, and began to crawl his way to shore. Amhuluk plunged his head below the water and the rest of his body flipped into the air to change course, like a snake.

"Hurry Jerrold," Marisol yelled. "Where's Dante?!"

Not too far from shore they could see bubbles coursing. Dante's head surfaced, just as Jerrold swam past him. They locked eyes for a moment. Then Dante was dragged below again.

"Oh no, oh no," Marisol cried. The confidence that she had gained over these few days was waning—Dante could really die. Jerrold breached the bank, his hands slapping onto the rocky surface, and Marisol pulled him up.

Amhuluk trapped Dante's leg in his mouth. Through the brackish water Dante could see Amhuluk's eyes. They were focused like a shark to blood. The serpent shook Dante, his body like a marionette, then he chuckled. His body looped in the water like seaweed.

"Amhuluk! You missed me!" Jerrold called.

"What are you doing!?" Marisol cried.

"We have to give Dante a chance to escape," Jerrold said. "I don't know what else to do!"

Underwater Dante noticed Amhuluk's eyes flicker toward the surface. With a *harrumph*, Amhuluk let Dante go. The serpent coursed toward the surface.

Dante swam like his lungs were popping. They were. He looped his arms like he knew how to swim. He didn't. It was clear to him that through their entire journey, this was the only moment he feared that he would die. He suddenly missed his parents.

Amhuluk breached the surface much faster than Dante. The 18-year-old gasped like he *had* been drowned when he reached fresh air. The serpent caught sight of Jerrold and shot his head toward the bank again.

Marisol grabbed the first thing she could to stop him. It was her doll. Jerrold saw Marisol's toy and dropped his bag to the floor. Like a mad man he unzipped it and took out his lacrosse stick. Marisol tossed him the doll, and he flung it in a big arc over the pool.

Amhuluk's razor eyes caught sight of the little person. His head and neck shot in the direction of the doll like a cell phone game of snake.

Marisol and Jerrold jumped into the water to help get Dante out. The doll plopped into the water off to Amhuluk's left, and the serpent drove his head down upon the toy, submerging it with the same dark glee with which he had submerged Dante. It didn't take long to get Dante out of the water, nor for Amhuluk to realize that he had been tricked.

The three now soaked travelers teetered away from the water, confused as to how to "free" Amhuluk. The serpent on the other hand was enraged, and grew to his full massive size above the water.

"What is this?! An idol? I drown *people* not trinkets!" he roared.

"We. . .just wanted. . .to help you," Marisol panted.

"Help me!? Help *me!?* I make the trees stand upside down. Wherever I go, the earth softens below me. I don't need help. I need only *game.*"

Amhuluk shot his head toward them, hoping to knock them into the water again, but they had scurried far enough away now that the creature only knocked aside his own feeding pole.

Amhuluk cried out and his bellow filled the underground world. Kobolds and Boqs from islands far away heard his cry, and knew to stay inside. The serpent thrashed, creating a great turbulence in the pool, and the three travelers helped each other walk up the path.

"We didn't do it," Dante gasped. "I feel so worthless."

Amhuluk slammed his body into the sides of his pool. He crashed and crashed into the wall, and a splinter ran up the side of the waterfall. Bam, bam, bam, and the stony wall began to fracture entirely. The wall itself seemed to soften, like a sponge absorbing water.

It split suddenly in two, a tremendous divide opening, and the water from the waterfall sputtered to a stop. It pooled at the mouth of the now torn asunder fall.

Big bones flung from the water freely as Amhuluk snaked himself in coils in the tiny lake. With the water churned, it was much clearer, and from their vantage point, the three could see just how big Amhuluk truly was. He barely fit in the pool. His wet, black eyes glared at them as they walked away.

Chapter 24

THEY LAY BESIDE THE enormous pile of garbage. It smelt bad, but it was as far as they could go before collapsing. They lay with their heads near each other, making an exhausted, water-logged flower.

"What the heck just happened?" Jerrold panted.

"Amhuluk," Marisol said. "Is *not* a prisoner. Those chains were for his victims, not for him."

"Why the *hell* would Coyote send us down there? I'm going to need some *serious* therapy!" Dante yelled.

Marisol stood up. The little houses on this island were chatting and chittering more than ever before, and many of the neighbors were out talking to each other. A few had even walked over to where the three of them rested to look out at the pool.

"Someone finally did it," one kobold said softly. "Escaped 'is clutches."

The little creature had big white eyes, and Marisol realized that he was blind. All the same, the kobold turned his head toward Marisol.

"'Ow'd ya do it, love? Escape the codger?"

"Oh," Marisol thought. "I had a doll. Amhuluk must have thought it was something else to drown."

"My, my," the kobold said quietly. "I should've sent me son out with one of them things. Never thought a'that. Huh."

The kobold turned and walked back inside. The conversations grew hushed, embarrassed almost, then faded. Marisol, Dante, and Jerrold picked themselves up and began to walk across back across the bridge.

No one was outside Eebee's house, so they continued on to the plaza. It was more alive than before, with lots of underground denizens chatting with each other outside Coyote's establishment.

They stormed in. A different band was playing, an odd distorted blue grass sound, and Coyote was behind the bar, as smiley as ever. His eyes swelled when he saw the three companions walking toward him.

"You're back! You're back? Wow," Coyote said. "I'm impressed. Salmon? Fry bread?"

"Yeah!" Jerrold cheered.

"Not now, Jerry," Dante said. "What the heck was going on down there? You did *not* give us all the pieces of the puzzle, dude."

Coyote whipped up the food faster than before. In less than a minute he somehow created a nearly identical plate of fish and oily fry bread, slamming the dishes down on the bar just like before.

"Dig in," Coyote said. "I bet you could use some food."

Marisol and Jerrold began to work away at the food, but Dante was not having it. He told Coyote what happened, how they had almost been drowned, and how Amhuluk had no chains on his neck.

"Well he's no wimp like Karrabad," Coyote said. "I think boxing fifteen grizzly bears would be easier than chaining up Amhuluk."

"I thought he was your friend!" Dante said. Marisol again wiped the plate with a bit of fry bread, as Jerrold eat the last bit of fish.

"That doesn't matter," Coyote waved his paw in the air to shoo away all the things he didn't care to hear about. "What matters is what he *did*. When you made him mad."

They told Coyote that Amhuluk had whipped around like a kid having a tantrum. That he had slammed into the wall.

"And? What happened to the wall?"

"It split. The waterfall stopped, uh, falling," Dante said.

The tall dog man clapped his paws and whistled. He tapped one of the kobolds this time, and again took off his apron. He walked into the storeroom and told the three to follow him, just like before. They sighed and followed him.

Under the uneven light of the torch, the three followed Coyote through the small room. In the back there was a door, and they followed him through it. Coyote began walking like a lawyer on his way to the biggest case of his life. They continued around the corner and through the plaza, the throngs of kobolds not paying any attention to the four.

"Could you please tell us what's going on?" Marisol asked.

"Look, I'll come clean: Amhuluk is a jerk. He came down here after they drained Wapato Lake in 1935. He came so that he wouldn't get any of the flak that was coming to him. I knew he'd try and drown you three."

"What!? Why did you send us there then!?" Marisol asked.

"I needed Amhuluk to destroy the waterfall! With no more water down here the bogs will finally be ready."

"Ready for what?" Dante asked.

"A revolution," Coyote grinned his big, toothy grin.

"So why haven't you done this already?" Marisol asked as they walked. "Why wait 'til now?" They could barely keep up with Coyote's enormous gait.

"I didn't want to be drowned, are you kidding me?" he said. "Plus, it's only *kind of* my jail down here. I could have left if I wanted. But I wanted to get the boqs out. They couldn't tell they were being imprisoned—the bogs miss the trees but they can't hardly tell that they are in prison at all. Karrabad gave them food and shelter, and they didn't know it was a trap until too late."

They were walking so fast Jerrold was half-jogging. Coyote took a sharp turn and walked down some earthen steps, cut like marble into the side of the wall of the island. He pointed his long arm toward the bottom of the ravine.

"See? The water is drying up." He pumped his fists in the air. "Yeeessssss!"

As they descended they could see that he was right. Each of the bridges spanned a long drop, but also a tributary, an underground river. But they were dwindling, and fast.

"The bogs are like anyone else," Coyote said. "They gotta drink. If they're jarred from their comforts, as meager as those have been, they'll be looking to get out of this dump."

"We didn't *want* to do you a favor. We wanted to get out," Marisol said.

"And now you can. Generous, aren't I? And thoughtful too, right?! *Thank you*, Coyote, *thank you*," Coyote said. "That's you. You were supposed to say those things."

"Ugh," Dante said. "How long until they'll be ready?"

The stairs reached a shelf. It was very small, but on their right was a door with a knob made of pure amethyst. Coyote rapped on it four times, *knock knock knockknock*, and pushed it open.

A barracks of bogs befell their sight. In bunk beds twenty deep there was a small army of huge, hairy men milling about. Some slept, some played cards at long coffee tables. They all drank the same grotto-y brew that Coyote had offered the three travelers.

"They're ready," Coyote said. "They just don't know it yet."

"Know what, boss?" a boq grumbled.

"That Amhuluk finally did it. He destroyed the waterfall. There's no more water."

A gasp and then silence fell over the throng. The card players dropped their cards, the sleepers hit their heads on the bunk beds as they sat up too fast, and the brew-drinkers dropped their brews. One particularly huge and messy boq threw up his fists:

"How are we going to take showers!?"

A *hear hear* escalated.

"And no more hot chocolate," Coyote pointed to the fallen mug.

An even louder resistance swelled.

"Is that what that was?" Dante whispered to Jerrold. He shrugged.

"Ya know what else," Marisol said loudly to the entire room.

Dante, Jerrold, and Coyote all whipped their heads to the fleece sporting girl. Countless eyes were pointed on her. She strode forward and climbed on top of one of the coffee tables.

"I miss the sun. I miss the crisp air of the woods. I miss the high trees and all of the animals of the forests." Her voice rose to a crescendo now as she addressed the full throng of bogs. "And I don't know about the rest of you, but more than anything else, I miss my *freedom*!"

She drove her fist in the air and the crowd exploded. Coyote smiled, water welling up in his eyes, and clapped excitedly. Dante and Jerrold cheered like they were at a football game.

The boqs started beating their chests and growling, pushing each other around and hollering. Coyote walked up to Marisol who was shouting and high fiving the increasingly amped up boqs.

"Hey girlie," Coyote said. "We gotta go."

"Why!? Everyone is so ready for revolution!"

"That's the problem. It's about to be a mad house in here. We'll be trampled."

"Just like Karrabad the oppressor will be trampled!" Marisol cheered.

"Right. Um, but we will literally be trampled," Coyote said.

"Oh," Marisol said, jumping down from the table. "Let's get going."

The four of them dashed out of the door, and sure enough a mass of boqs flooded from the amethyst door. They ran as fast as they could, only a few feet separating them from the horde. Up the stairs they climbed as the tidal wave surged. On the last few steps Coyote grabbed Marisol and Jerrold and flung them over the side, and Dante jumped up and over. The pounding of boqs blew past them and forward, onto the bridge headed away from the now emptied pool.

"Where are they going?!" Marisol asked.

"Up," Coyote said. "To Karrabad."

"Up? There's a way to just *walk* out of here?"

"How do you think the kobolds do it?" Coyote said. "We'd better hurry. Who knows if Karrabad has used the sword yet."

He took off toward the next bridge with Dante, Jerrold, and Marisol closely in tow.

Chapter 25

"ARE THE KOBOLDS GOING to revolt, too?" queried Jerrold. "They can't like Karrabad very much if he enslaves them."

"Those colonized tend to stay pretty dormant as long as they're content. Karrabad is the evil they know—unless something happens directly to them, they'll just keep on keeping on. They're fat and happy, who can blame them?"

"Me," Marisol said. "I can. That's just dumb."

"You're sharp," Coyote said. "And feisty too." Winking at her. "I like that!"

The last bridge was almost destroyed after the boqs stormed over it, but they did managed to cross. A huge tunnel opened before them, gently rising up and to the left.

"Those boqs were really fast," Jerrold said. "But I don't think we can go as fast as them. We fell for a *really* long time."

"I can get us up there faster," Coyote grinned. "Hold on. I won't need these anymore, stupid kobolds."

He tore off his clothes. The three travelers looked away, but he was, after all, a coyote, and it wasn't too startling. He dropped to all fours and stretched his back like a cat, his eyes glimmering yellow. It was an ancient and powerful thing.

Dante noticed it first. His shoes were unlacing like they were melting, and turning a rich ochre. The muscles in his ankles tightening, strengthening.

Marisol looked at her feet and saw the same thing—her shoes were almost black, and shrinking. They were wrapping around her feet, and her feet were shrinking, too.

It was Jerrold who put it together:

"Do we have hooves?!"

"Quiet now, Jerrold," Coyote said. He still was on his paws like a true coyote, channeling his powers. "It'll be over in juuuuust a second."

With a snap like dry wood splitting, their amorphous black feet split down the middle. Each of them looked like satyrs now; their legs had narrowed just below the calf and become like the legs of mountain sheep.

"We'd better get going," Coyote stood again, his eyes mellowing. "Those boqs sure are fast."

"How is this supposed to make us go faster?" Dante asked. He stamped his feet in place, his patience wearing thin.

"You tell me," Coyote said. "You know, you don't tell *me* very much at all. Sort of selfish, McCormick, if you ask me."

Like a slender ghost he bounded away. It seemed like walking with him earlier had been him at his absolute slowest. He was disappearing deep up into the dark tunnel almost immediately.

Marisol started to follow, and she realized that each of her steps was like a bounce. She was racing without even trying, each step flinging her like she was crossing a mountain pass. Then she really tried to run, and she was gone.

"Oh jeeze," Jerrold said. "Okay, here I go."

Jerrold zipped ahead, and Dante followed right behind. They caught up to Marisol and all three clipped into the dark. Totally unafraid, entirely determined. It was the same feeling they'd had leaving home, the same when they decided to travel together, the same when they decided to trust Howard at the Ore-gone-ian, and the same they had when they first entered Brewer's Yawn.

It was taking the first step. That was the key. That gave the power. The only difference now was that their steps were with cloven feet.

The ascent was steep at first, but it became absolutely vertical before long. They looked up and saw a light. From down here it was just a pinhole, but it was light.

A shadow danced through the light. It zig-zagged back and forth like a vigilante hopping from roof to roof. They saw that it was Coyote, making his way from shelf to shelf in quick bounds.

"That's like Mario," Jerrold said. "Wall jump."

"Not *now*, Jerry!" Dante said. "Wait. No, you're right, that's *exactly* what it's like."

Marisol went first. She squatted down and used all her might to leap into the air toward the first bit of rock. Without a thought she leapt from there to the next shelf, Coyote's gifts working like magic. Which, in fact, of course they were.

Dante and Jerrold followed. They laughed as they went, their newly-hoofed feet doing all the work to connect them from wall to wall. It was a lot more fun than falling.

The light swelled and swelled like a solar flare. As they ascended, it was like flying toward the sky, even though they knew that it was just another layer of underground. Their world was still a-ways to go.

Marisol jumped from the last ledge to the cave floor.

"How did the boqs pull this off?" Jerrold asked.

"They seem pretty good at this kind of stuff," Dante said. "This is their world, after all."

They found themselves in a smallish room with only one door heading out. Simpler to direct enslaved kobolds in one direction rather than to confuse them with two.

The three spelunkers extraordinaire walked toward it, and as they went they felt their hooves grow toes. The colors of their shoes began to repurpose themselves. Their legs returned to the way they'd been before. Jerrold wiggled his toes in his shoes just to make sure they were still there.

"That's the way to go," he said. "I can see it. There's a party going on in there."

They neared the door when Dante stopped.

"Hey," Dante said. "Before we go in there."

Marisol and Jerrold stopped and looked at Dante. He was looking at his hands, which he fidgeted in front of him.

"You both saved me," he said quietly.

"Ah, Ahmuluk was a jerk, and Coyote kind of, too. It was nothing," Jerrold smiled.

"No. You saved me when we met at the bus stop. And again in the park in Bend. And again at Howard's house when you let me mess up. I'm. . .I'm so glad I've met you both."

Marisol and Jerrold were speechless. It had been an overwhelming time for all three of them, but Dante was making it so real.

"I know I've learned a lot," Jerrold said. "About myself. About who I am, who I'm becoming. I couldn't have done it without either of you."

"Yeah. And I know I can make huge changes in my life. There's esperanza for me, and for all of us. You helped us see that, Dante."

He wiped a tear from his eyes. It mingled with the left over water of the pool, but they could tell all the same. He extended his arms like a saint, his head still hanging. Marisol and Jerrold gave him a tremendous hug, and his head rose like a flower lifting itself to the sun.

Chapter 26

THE FINAL DOOR WAS wider, and looked like the edges had been blown apart. Little bits of stone littered the path. In the distance they heard yelling and brawling.

"I hope Karrabad hasn't used the sword yet," Dante said. "Though I can't imagine how his little hands would."

"They're so tiny," Marisol said.

"Don't get too excited," Jerrold said. "I can see a lot of commotion."

The door led to a short tunnel. After what they had just gone through, *all* tunnels seemed like short tunnels. The noises grew, and when they entered the ultimate room, it was like entering a war zone.

The chamber was the same one that they had found King Karrabad in before, the same one that they had fallen from. Spread out across the floor were boqs and kobolds fighting like soldiers in some great battle. For each boq there were three or four kobolds clinging to their huge arms, clambering up their backs, stabbing at their hairy legs. Bodies were already strewn around like a mausoleum.

A kobold flew over their heads, and they had to dodge to avoid getting smacked.

"Sorry," a boq called. "But be careful!"

They ran behind a stalagmite to gather their bearings. They heard a barking and yelling, and began to look for Coyote. The madness was embroiling, but Marisol gingerly stepped forward.

Dante and Jerrold struggled to keep up with her as they crossed the granite earth. Kobolds ran toward them, their eyes much angrier than Eebee's, and it broke their hearts to kick them away like mangy animals.

"This is horrible," Jerrold said. "What's going on at the back? Where's the sword?"

A tall man stood at the rear of the room. When they looked closer they saw it was a human sized kobold. He had long white robes with silver running down the middle. A long curved sword rested in his perfectly normal sized hands. An eyepatch covered one of his bloody eyes. It was King Karrabad in his humanoid form.

"Kids!" Coyote called. He was standing in front of the elegant kobold and his eyes were that mystical yellow once more. "Karrabad's almost done healing, and he's getting ready to leave the cave! I need your help!"

King Karrabad raised the sword in front of him like a commander, and out of thin air tiny daggers began to form like snow. They flew toward Coyote. The Kalapuyan guardian raised big earthen tendrils from the floor and knocked the daggers aside with big, powerful, earthen whips.

With a twist of the sword, King Karrabad took control of Coyote's constructs. They turned against Coyote now and began to encircle their former master. They pinned him to the floor and chained him, just like Karrabad had been chained to the wall before.

"Talapus, prankster protector of the Kalapuyan people," the king's voice echoed in their minds. "With the sword added to my psychic abilities, you have no hope of imprisoning me again. It's taken hundreds of years, but I am nearly ready to fly. Your world will soon be mine."

The three travelers stood frozen. The voices of countless angry boqs and kobolds stormed behind them, and the demise of their hopes lay directly in front of them.

"Hey!" Coyote yelled, writhing against the tightening stone. "A little help here?"

"There's nothing we can do," Jerrold shouted over the cacophony. "What are we supposed to do?"

"Hold on," Marisol said. "This is the perfect moment. Karrabad jut said it. He's not ready." She looked into each of her companion's eyes.

"But we are," Dante said. "So there's still a chance. A little help might be exactly what we have to offer."

Dante and Marisol charged forward, but Jerrold was still rooted. That's when he realized how *he* could help. He closed his eyes, and breathed deeply. When he opened his eyes he had tapped even further into the cave, and everything that had been in it for too long.

"Karrabad's redirected his energy to his body," Jerrold said. "But his brain is still the source of his power. Just do what you were going to do before, Dante."

Marisol rushed ahead of Dante and straight at the king, in all of his newfound saintly glory. With a smirk he flicked the tip of the sword and Marisol was tossed to the right like she was the muñeca. This distraction gave Dante his opportunity.

For every time he had said no, for every time he shut the world out, for every moment he missed with Martha, he lunged into Karrabad. The king was focusing in too many places at once, and he took the full tackle. They fell to the stone, and the king clunked his head. Hard.

"Foolish boy! It's always been you. Denying me," the king held onto the sword. "No longer."

Dante rose in the air, psionically lifted by the king. As he began to float, he reached down and grabbed the hilt of the sword. King Karrabad's own power to toss Dante around like he was nothing is precisely what made him lose the sword.

Realizing his folly, the King bent over to scoop up the sword, dropping Dante in the process. Dante jumped to his feet and head-butted the kobold overlord, hitting him squarely in the middle of his face. As the king recoiled, Dante grabbed the sword and stepped back to gave himself room for a proper stance.

"Now, Dante," Jerrold spoke in Dante's mind.

Marisol saw the goings on from the stalagmite that she had been thrown into, and she gave two thumbs up. Like a knight, Dante swung the sword down in a beautiful, powerful arc.

It sunk deep into the king's exposed, Frankenstein brain.

The radio shrieking from before grew and shattered the room. The boqs doubled over, crying out and grabbing their fuzzy heads. The kobolds all fell to the ground writhing. Their eyes lost any tint of red, becoming the simple whites and blues and yellows that they once were.

Coyote found freedom as the stoney chains disassembled into pebbles and powdery earth. He staggered to his feet, then threw his hands to his head and howled with pain. Jerrold and Marisol were crying out, too, but Dante, despite the terrible noise, kept his sword steady.

As he withdrew the bloody blade, King Karrabad's now limp body fell with a dull thud. The blaring siren of sound peaked quickly then faded completely away. The only noises left were the scattered moans and groans.

Boqs helped kobolds stand, and the kobolds tended to boq wounds. The great battle was over.

"Hey," Coyote panted. "Great work, kid. You're a natural."

Dante felt weak. He didn't feel proud — it wasn't anything to be proud of. It felt like Howard drowning the rabid kobold in the creek. The killing just had to happen. And he had been the one who had to do it.

"Thanks," Dante said. He didn't have any extra words. He looked at the sword in his hands. He wanted to leave the weapon in the cave forever.

Jerrold ran to Marisol and helped her up. She smiled shakily.

"You're so brave, Marisol," Jerrold said, linking his arm underneath hers.

"I think we all are," Marisol said. "Esperanza. I think my back is really messed up though."

Coyote leapt up on top of a stalagmite and stood like a ballerina mid-pirouette. He turned to the boqs and the kobolds and stretched his arms out like a saint.

"Germans and Natives, kobolds and boqs," he smiled. "May I present. . .your freedom!"

Instant applause flooded the vaulting chamber like a tsunami. Kobolds cried and hugged each other, boqs lifted each other in huge hugs, and kobolods hugged boqs' legs en masse while the boqs bent down and passed around tiny hugs.

"It wasn't me that won you your freedom this day," Coyote continued. "May I present, Marisol, Jerrold, and Dante." The applause grew even louder. "If it weren't for the trials and tribulations these three surmounted, we'd all still be waiting for the day that big lump came a knocking on our doors."

The cheers grew higher and higher as Marisol, Jerrold, and Dante all took respective bows. Dante was crying a bit, and Jerrold and Marisol patted him on the back like he had some form of indigestion.

"You *did* it, Dante," Jerrold winked.

"Not. . .alright Jerry, thanks," Dante said.

Coyote bent into his animal stance and turned his eyes that same powerful yellow. He howled and the cave began to shake again. Instead of any cracks or holes or traps, things began to repair. In the war-torn room a warmth grew, filling the cold. Lifeless kobolds and boqs began to have their wounds healed. Their eyes fluttered to life, then they sucked air into their lungs.

A long oak table spread along the wall and sprouted all sorts of drinks and foods. Roasted meat and vegetables, cakes as high as the stone ceiling, and bowls of punch that had *no* business being in a cave.

In a flash a three-piece kobold band, with a boq bassist, appeared in the center of the room. They had the finest instruments in Oregon, Coyote made sure.

And as they began to play, and as the healing went into full swing, the world further below started to churn. The riven in the wall patched itself like a spider spinning web through rock, and Amhuluk watched as water began to dribble. The malevolent force cracked a smile as the waterfall roiled to life.

Coyote, Marisol, Jerrold, and Dante all danced in the middle of the room, hugging and grinning, their wounds a thing of the past. For the three travelers, so much of their pasts were no able to be left comfortably in the past.

Chapter 27

THE PARTY LASTED SEVERAL hours. It flashed by like a fantastic dream. Nobody ended up dying, except for one tyrant, and, quite the contrary, none of the combatants had ever felt so alive. The kobolds went back to their homes below, and the boqs sailed out of the caverns through the path that the fishies had created with the sword.

At the mouth of the cave, Coyote stopped the group of wildsfolk.

"Despite all of my many pranks, I love each and every one of you. Deeply. You are my family these many, many years," he paused, scanning the assembled group. "I'm so glad you're above ground again—back where you belong."

"I don't think we ever knew what had become of us," one said, scratching her head. "It happened so slowly over so much time."

"You can't be blamed," Coyote assured her. "That's exactly how it was designed to go."

They waved goodbye to their new friends, and still moving as one huge mass the great throng of bogs exited Brewer's Yawn for good. Coyote and the teens walked back into the room where Karrabad had been shackled.

"What will you do with the body?" Coyote asked one of the kobolds. He wore a helmet on his scaly head that made him look like the world's tiniest Viking.

"We was hopin' *you* might do somefin' wif him," he shrugged. "It's no good of us a'take him back below. 'E'll be crucified."

"Yeesh," Coyote said. "Alright. Well, we'll do it then."

He loaded the body over his shoulder and turned for the door. Marisol lifted the sword, tossed it in between her hands, and gripped the hilt.

"Doesn't that freak you out?" Jerrold asked.

"No," Coyote said. "Death is just as necessary as life, kid. Admittedly I'm quite a bit older than you are, but you just get used to it over time."

They followed him out. Walking out of the cave felt lighter than ever, a literal breath of fresh air. As Dante walked, he felt his burden lift, and everyone gave each other all the space they needed. They intermittently chatted about their final battle, and the insane adventures they'd had in just the past few days.

Coyote walked into the Deschutes Forest first. It was late afternoon, a mellow sun hung in the sky like a bloated peach. He lay the remarkably man-looking Karrabad down against a tree and bent into his fox stance. As he channeled his power, a plot of land in front of the Yawn began to spin into existence. The dirt wheeled around and away from the rectangle. A proper hole, with excellent walls, was constructed in front of the mouth of the cave.

Coyote picked up Karrabad and knelt down by the hole, carrying the late King like a rescued princess. He lay him in the hole, his long arms reaching down to the bottom.

"Why are we burying him again?" Dante asked.

"There's a sacredness to the dead," Marisol whispered.

"I want to heal the land," Coyote said. "He ate the food of this forest, probably any ways, and now his body will become food for it in turn. Sort of poetic, right?"

Dante and Jerrold nodded as Coyote filled the hole again with earth. It didn't take a very long time at all. Marisol took the sword in her hands and made a concha appear out of the air, smelling sweet and pristine, then some flowers and sugar skulls. They decorated the plot like he had been family. Which, to some, he may have been.

"Alright," Coyote sighed. "That's it for me. I'm glad you kids found me down there. My passion for small business was overpowering my interest in liberating my kinsfolk, I guess. Heck, I too had become used to the shut in life we'd been living."

"You're ridiculo, Coyote," Marisol said. "Thanks for helping us stop King Karrabad."

"Seriously," Dante said. "We wouldn't have been able to do it without you."

"I know I learned a lot," Jerrold said, his eyes far away. "Down there. But don't try and drown anybody else, would'ja?"

Coyote laughed, cackled, and howled at the same time, his body bending like a scarecrow's. He dabbed at his eyes, pretending to wipe tears away.

"You kids are so inspiring," Coyote said. "In seriousness—something I almost never am in so pay attention—you three, your presence, ended up being just as important as me down there today. Don't forget that."

They didn't know what to say—it wasn't until much later that they even agreed with him.

"What are you going to do with that thing now? Dropping it down a hole you and your friends dig is, apparently, not enough to keep it satisfied."

"We'll figure out something," Marisol said. "We have so far."

Coyote smiled and dipped his chin in a sort of bow. He turned to leave and they saw his full frame against the sun. His long gait put him a good distance away from them rather quickly. Over his shoulder he called out,

"And tell Howard that his great-grandpappy was a good guy, a real decent fellow for an explorer type. Tell him that his sketch of me was spot on—I had nicer hair though, and I think a sharper jawline. But what do I know." A parting wink over his shoulder, and he was gone.

Their eyes swelled as Coyote faded from vision. Dante fell to the ground, *ugh*ing his way down. Then he spun and faced the cave. The other two watched him as he just sat and thought. They sat down by him, Jerrold resting his head against Dante's shoulder, Marisol laying an arm around them both.

It was the kind of moment that signifies the end of a camping trip, or the classic first night on a college campus. The type of unification people go to work retreats to try and conjure—it was an unspeakable ease.

"Now that King Karrabad is gone," Dante finally said. "I want to try to close Brewer's Yawn again."

He extended the sword toward Marisol. His eyes were cast down, like he had just messed up.

"I think that's a good idea. His powers won't be blocking the cave anymore," Marisol nodded. "So go for it, Dante."

"What?"

"Go ahead and close it," Marisol said. "You showed us you can use the sword. So go for it."

"I," Dante stammered. "I guess I could try."

Dante stood and stepped beyond Karrabad's grave, in between the plot and the mouth. His hands clasped the hilt and he spread his feet, like

Marisol always does. He breathed, and cleared his mind like he had inside the cave.

Thoughts of King Karrabad and his parents and Martha all flooded him once he shut his eyes. But he just watched the thoughts go by. A few tears pressurized out of his eyes, but he just let them arc around his face and course to the ground.

A rush of air spread around his body like a cyclone. Jerrold grinned. Dante's eyes spread open and were full of electricity. Marisol folded her arms and just smiled.

The cave undulated like a bag of popcorn being popped, jumping and shaking randomly across its top. They could hear a rumbling from deep within. Stalagmites and stalactites and all kinds of -ites shattered and crashed as the mouth of the cave began to waver. Reality was undone by the sword just in the same way it was unraveled just a few days before.

The cave shrunk to a hill, then to a mound, and within moments it was gone. Dante squeezed tighter, and the felled trees and shrubs rolled back into their holes. Their roots now stronger than ever.

"Well done, my man," Jerrold said.

The air and the power died down, like night after a storm, and Dante fell to the earth.

"Ugh," he said. "That's hard! Did it work, though?"

"Yeah," Marisol said. "It's like the Yawn was never here. We'd better go, though. There's no way people won't notice that the cave that just appeared, just disappeared."

They helped Dante stand and began to walk away. The earth felt a lot better below their feet instead of over their heads. The sky welcomed them home.

"Wait," Dante said. "I think we have to do something. Right now."

Marisol and Jerrold looked at Dante. His eyes filled with a strong conviction.

"Let's get rid of the sword," Dante said. "Like they did in Howard's family journal."

"Why?!" Jerrold asked. "We can do so much good with it! Remember what we made for that school?"

Marisol looked at the sword in the lowlight. She listened as her friends debated. It glimmered like a star, throwing light in a multitude of thin, brilliant beams.

"There's a way to do this right," Marisol said. She asked for the sword. Dante surrendered it, his hands sky bound in haplessness.

Marisol firmly grasped the sword and channeled its powers. This time it was a bit different—all the light and power swirled around the blade itself, forming a small whirlwind that pinwheeled over the gem on the sword. In no time at all, the jewel burst.

"What is she doing?!" Jerrold yelled.

"Don't second guess her, Jerry," Dante said. "She knows exactly what she's doing."

The fragments of the stone flew in separate directions like dust, and then the blade began to quake and fall apart, too. That grippy, familiar hilt was the only thing grounded in the small hurricane that Marisol was creating.

Just as the blade exploded, it began to reclaim itself. The fragments were sucked back to the hilt of the sword, swirling still like a faerie's breath. An orb of light began to grow from Marisol and the sword. The brightness forced both Jerrold and Dante had to look away.

When the light faded and they could see again, they saw Marisol standing in that familiar pose. She looked like a vigilant knight, a powerful bruja. In her hands she held three small tools.

"Okay, I made the sword into three new things. I think this will be much better. I hope that's okay with you two."

"I was confused for a second, but If you think it's a good idea," Jerrold said. "Then I'm on board."

"Yeah," Dante said. "That works better than throwing the thing down a well."

"Dante, this one's for you," Marisol said. She handed him a pendant, the same color and shape as the sword's original jewel. A leather string looped through a tiny hole at the top.

Dante slid it over his neck. When it fell across his chest, he felt that same power from the sword radiating across his skin.

"I thought of it because you have been reflecting so much," Marisol said. "It seemed like the right thing for you."

Dante smiled, nodded. He grasped the jewel and felt a rush he had never felt while using the sword.

"Jerrold, I made you a spy glass," Marisol said. It was silver like the metal of the blade, and the size of Jerrold's palms put back to back. It too had the same ring of power that the pendant held.

He peered through it and smiled.

"For seeing?"

"Yeah," Marisol said.

"What about for you, Marisol?" Dante asked.

She showed them a black dagger, the same color of the now gone hilt. It looked like a black unicorn horn, with a spiral pattern running up and down its length.

"I always felt so connected to the sword," Marisol said. "I thought some kind of smaller version of it might be right."

"Seems right to me," Jerrold said. "Totally fine. This way we can still use the powers, but maybe in more sustainable ways?"

"Like superpowers," Marisol said. "Without anyone collapsing."

They laughed. It was like they finally could breathe freely and deeply, appreciate the woods, enjoy the world. The three stood next to each other and marveled at what Marisol had made for them. They had never felt so connected to each other.

Chapter 28

THEY WALKED INTO THE town's cell phone range and, again risking their airplane-less phones, ordered a Lyft. Some other frustrated college graduate gave them a ride through the densely packed trees. They didn't talk much, not wanting to explore their journey in front of a total stranger.

It was a good thing that they didn't have the sword anymore—without its shawl sheath it was pretty hard to hide a scimitar with an enormous jewel in its blade.

Instead of going to downtown Bend they went instead directly to Casa de Shannibald. Deano and Lilly were running alongside the car as soon as the driver hit the dirty path, and it wasn't long before he said that he had gone far enough.

"Can't you walk from here?" he asked.

"Yes," Marisol said. "We paid you to take us to the door, though."

The driver groaned and continued on. The Honda Accord finally stopped in front of the door.

"Don't forget to give me a five-star rating," he said.

Marisol said nothing as Dante and Jerrold mumbled sounds of assent. They took their freshly-Coyote healed selves and their bags and exited the car.

Howard and Shanna were already waiting on the porch, their arms around each other more for security's sake than affection. Their faces were painted half with panic and half with elation to see the kids again.

"Oh my god," Shanna said. "You were gone so long!"

They ran to the steps as the Honda pulled away. They hugged and were a family again, a group of traveling fish back in their school. The dogs yipped and ran in circles, like a pack of firecrackers popping off.

Inside they sat at the table and told the older couple all about their meeting with King Karrabad, how he stopped them and sent them to his chambers below, the world of the kobolds and the guardians trapped below, and the final battle that ensued. They told them what they had done with the sword.

Jerrold scarfed cookies the whole time, and fed a few to the pups as they scooted around.

"Coyote, eh?"

"He says that your great-grandpappy was a cool guy," Dante said.

"I'll be damned," Howard said. "Fascinating, fascinating!"

"Can we see your new tools? You were gone so long I was worried we wouldn't ever see you again."

Jerrold showed his spy glass.

"We weren't gone too long," Jerrold said. "We needed a few hours to. . .learn more about ourselves, ya know?"

Shanna's brow furrowed, then arced into two surprised apostrophes.

"A *few* hours? You were gone for almost a day and a half, Jerrold."

Jerrold almost spit out his cookies, though didn't, and Marisol gasped.

"Over twenty-four hours?" Dante asked. "Time moves really weird down there."

Howard sat down and exhaled.

"We almost had to call your parents," he said.

Marisol stood up, and Dante slammed the table. Jerrold *did* spit his cookie out.

"But you didn't, right!?"

"A full day, and then some, is a long time when you're talking about someone else's kids," Shanna said. "It's been almost a week since the first time Howard sat with you all on the patio. It has to come to an end at some point."

Marisol and Jerrold looked uneasy, but Dante kept a straight face. He flickered to his phone for a second, tossing it in his hand, then shoved it back in his pocket.

"That's why we like you," Dante said. "Playing it cool. We'll figure it out. Thanks for trusting us."

Shanna and Howard looked at each other quickly, then smiled.

"Well, glad we figured that out," Shanna said. "Anyone want to help me figure out dinner? I was thinking a big bone broth stew."

"That sounds sort of Amhuluk-ish," Jerrold said. "I'm going to go outside for a while. Just to, ya know, get some fresh air."

He and Marisol both walked outside, headed toward the Secret Place, while Dante stayed inside to help dice veggies. In so many ways it felt as though nothing enormous had happened, just a week full of the normal stuff in life. But all five of them knew that this wasn't really so, and each one decided to make changes in their lives in own ways.

Chapter 29

THEIR DINNER WAS A stewy affair that rang *nothing* of Amhuluk, except that maybe the broth looked a bit like brackish water. This was the boiled kale's fault though.

After dinner, everyone went on a long walk around the property, tinkering with their new totems. Marisol, the creator adept, formed a few tiny muñecas out of gravel and let them dissolve again, simply by swishing her dagger in the air. Jerrold brought two squirrels in a nearby tree together to share their acorns. Dante used his pendant to make flowers bloom at night.

The moon hung over them like a friendly old scholar, winking as they did their best through the rabble of life. Shanna and Howard told them stories of when *they* were their age, how they had taken off from home to scout out the Midwest and the South. How both had been miraculous places of snow and sun, but something brought them back home.

"Hard to beat the West Coast," Howard smiled.

"West Coast, Best Coast," Shanna said.

Back at the house they slept in the same arrangements as before. Marisol fell asleep faster than anyone, her wounds having been healed but her exhaustion still at an all-time high. Dante and Jerrold chatted a bit into the night, talking about the new ways that they saw themselves, the new ways that they saw others.

When they woke up, it was like an impasse had been crossed. Marisol began by telling them that on her walk to the Secret Place she had decided to switch on her phone. It was clogged with over forty messages and voicemails from her brothers, mom, and dad. She had decided to call her mom.

Jerrold said the same thing. He had been wandering and feeling like taking that important step—facing front with his folks. They deserved to know what he had been learning about himself on his adventure over these last seven days.

"I can't believe you called your parents!" Dante said.

"I really missed them, Dante," Jerrold said.

"No, it's okay," Dante said, a smile spreading on his face. "I called mine, too."

"You dog! Stand up, Dante, stand up! A long career in comedy for this one."

They laughed, and Marisol joined in, laughing louder than the other two had ever seen her laugh. Howard and Shanna smiled with their arms tight-knit around each other. They all loaded into the Subaru and drove back into the woods. Each of the kids had told their parents that they had been camping with their new friends, and that they wanted to enjoy the last bit of time in the woods while they could.

Three sentinel vehicles sat revving in the parking lot at the head of the Yawn's old trail. Howard parked the Subaru near the other three, and the flood gates opened. Each kid ran over to their tribe, saying thanks to Howard and Shanna as they jumped out.

It was like seeing three animals returning home, despite being in the middle of the woods. The units glommed on to each other immediately.

Jerrold's parents jumped out of their Prius faster than Jerrold had ever seen them move. He had the spy glass in his front pocket, but his parents must not have noticed as they all hugged.

"Hey," he looked up at both of them. "You took the Prius!"

They wore trembling smiles and tears in the corners of their eyes. It was like they were seeing a deer on the side of the highway, so careful not to scare the gentle thing that they had the food fortune to come upon. Then they hugged their kid, and the three laughed. Jerrold stepped back for a moment.

"What is it, son?" his dad squeaked.

"That's sort of the thing. I'm not your son," Jerrold said. "I'm not sure where I'm at, but I'm not that right now."

"That's fine, Jerry," his mom said. "That's just totally fine."

Dante's parents were just as ecstatic to see him. His father wrapped his arms around him and sobbed, while his mother threw her arms around them both, smiling.

"I didn't know what to do about Martha," Dante cried. "I wanted to do something about Martha."

"It's alright, son," his mother said, her voice a hush. "We know."

Dante's pendant around his neck shimmered as the three of them grieved.

It was Marisol's family that wasn't entirely up to snuff. Her brothers all rushed to her side, talking fast like they had years to catch up on. Her mother was quivering as Marisol walked up to them. But her father seemed angry.

"No lo puedo creer," he said. "How could you leave your family?"

All of her brothers rushed out to hug her, and Marisol grinned. Her father remained stoic, not budging.

"I can't *believe* you, Santos," Lutecia said. She shoved past her husband and joined the kids in loving on the recently MIA Marisol. There in the dark of the woods, Santos put a few things together. He lumbered over to his family, and he apologized. With that, they brought him into the group hug, too.

Shanna and Howard had gone for a walk to give some room, and came back in time to catch them at their final moment. They had called all of their families on the first day they were at Casa de Shannibald. They had explained that if they didn't give the kids a chance to write their own stories, the three families might never have their kids home again. The next few days rolled on with their blessings, though Howard and Shanna didn't mention any magical swords or cave-dwelling rodent people.

Howard stuck his hand out for Dante, who grabbed it and shook it hard.

"Good luck, fishes," Howard said. "It's been a treat to get to know the three of you."

"And no hard feelings about calling your parents?" Shanna asked.

"No," Marisol said. "We get it. We did what we had to do, and y'all did what you had to do."

"It seems like it all worked out okay," Howard said. "And they don't know about the...powers, right?"

"No," Dante said. "That might get us all put on permanent house arrest."

Howard and Shanna laughed, while Deano and Lilly barked from inside the Subaru.

"We'd better get these two home," Shanna said.

"Come visit us anytime," Howard said. "You have our numbers right?"

"We have 'em," Jerrold said. "Make sure to put a plate of cookies out for me every night, so when I'm lost in the woods I'll follow my nose and know which way to go!"

Dante's handshake finally escalated into a full-blown hug. Marisol hopped in to hug both Howard and Shanna at the same time, as tightly as she could. Jerrold came in and hugged Howard, then Shanna, too. The five-person company held each other for just a little while. Their quest had come finally to a close.

The water was on fire with sunlight. The three sat with their legs dangling over the bank of the Drake River. They had asked their parents for a final afternoon together before heading back to their regular lives. Not that they could ever do that, but what did their parents know?

"It's so pretty," Jerrold said. "Look at that remote controlled ship. A ship that is remote controlled!"

"It's not like Oakland up here," Marisol said. "I wish I'd had more time to sit around and enjoy this place."

"We can come back someday," Dante said.

Jerrold and Marisol smiled at him. They'd exchanged numbers, just in case.

"I mean, why not? I've got my pendant, Jerrold's got his spy glass, and Marisol with your dagger, there's no *way* we couldn't make this work. The real question would be, should we?"

"Why do you say that?" Marisol asked.

"We can make our lives better now," Dante said. "We already have."

A large boat passed in front of them all as the warm glow of sun kept on kissing their faces.

"But we have to, ya know, *try*, too," Dante said. "If I learned anything from King Karrabad, it's that these tools aren't for 'magic-ing' the world into a better place. We have to do things for ourselves."

"I guess you're right," Jerrold said. "It would make things easier."

"Hey, I won't tell you not to make yourself some peanut butter cookies, Jerry. But I know I have to go back to school—finish up."

"I thought you were done with school?" Marisol asked.

"Not really," he threw a big chunk of charred something into the water from the bank. "I can get my GED, though. I want to start working with this nonprofit in town."

"That seems like a good idea," Jerrold said. "I know I'm going to head back with my parents, too. I think they realized how much I was sort of hating school, and they said we just have too much privilege to have such a bad thing going on. I guess I'm going to be homeschooled for a little bit."

"Really?" Dante asked. "Are you about that, though?"

"Sort of. I said I wanted to see a therapist. That'll be cool. Beats lacrosse, am I right?"

They both laughed. Marisol just looked out at the sun.

"I think I will, too," she finally said. "Go back to school, I mean. I really love coding, almost as much as I love pottery, and I think that this whole thing, all the power of the sword, has shown me that I can be proud to make what I want to happen, actually happen. I don't need to be afraid of making a change anymore."

She took the dagger from her pocket. She grasped it tight and, with not a ripple of wind or a flash of light to be seen, she made a couple of tiny ant hills rise on the bank in front of them like a semi-circle. Little ants fled from the top like ball bearings out of a chute.

They all sunk when she let it go.

"With King Karrabad gone we all have to just move on," she said. "Which seems like a good thing. It's a good thing, right?"

"Not a problem for me," Jerrold said. "That guy was as scary as a scorned prom date!"

"You've never even been to the prom, Jerry," Dante smiled.

"And at this rate I never will! But I can dream," Jerrold said, propping his hands under his chin like a princess.

The three walked back to their tribes. Even Santos was happy to see the trio, and each family said their farewells. The parents exchanged contact information, trading numbers and social media info while the three travelers made a plan.

"Group chat? Make sure we all stay on the straight and narrow?" Dante asked.

"For sure," Jerrold said. "And we meet here at The Ore-gone-ian next year? For recon purposes only, of course."

"Por su puesto," Marisol said. "And your artifacts are safe?"

Dante took his pendant out from under his sweater, and Jerrold flashed the spy glass.

"Good," Marisol said. "We found esperanza out here."

"What's that mean?" Jerrold asked.

"Hope," Marisol smiled.

"Oh, we found that for sure," Dante said. "And all in just one little week. We turned things around in just a week! We *did* it."

They hugged each other, another group hug, and laughed in between tears. Even though it had only been a short few days, it was hard to think that their trust circle would have to grow by so many miles.

Marisol got in her family's van, Jerrold in the Prius, and Dante in his parent's Escalade. As they drove away, they felt their artifacts pulling on each other, trying to get close again. They knew it wouldn't be very long until they would come back to the Deschutes Forest.

Chapter 30

DANTE WOKE UP TO the sound of his mother's voice that carried like a sailing breeze. It was much better than an iPhone alarm, and he much preferred it.

"'Morning, Mom," Dante said as he came down the stairs.

"Good morning, Dante," Belinda said. "Are you going by today?"

"Yeah I'll make a stop. Want me to grab some flowers?"

"Yes please, that'd be lovely," Belinda said. "We'll be eating around 6:30."

"No problem, I'll be home way before that," Dante grabbed his backpack. "See ya."

"Bye, Dante!"

Tacoma had become a much better place since Dante got back two months ago. It wasn't a night and day kind of thing, the untrained eye might not catch the differences, but things had gotten better.

He drove the Cutlass Sierra to school and went to first period. Then second, then third, then fourth. He had found school to be a lot better now that he could breathe. Clearing his mind, releasing some of those scarier thoughts, and relaxing.

"Wanna go out later, Dante?" Michael asked him in fifth period. "I know a place we can score."

Dante cleared his mind, took a breath, and responded:

"Michael, you know I haven't done that stuff since Martha died. Since even *before* Martha died. You really should stop asking me about it, man."

"I'm sorry," Michael said. "You're my best friend. I don't mean to put you on the spot or nothin'."

"It's alright," Dante smiled. "Just food for thought."

He had quit the gelato job, but had left Roger with an entire freezer full of perfectly made pans of gelato, all the cocoa powder and Oreo bits he would ever need, and a brand new freezer-mixer. Roger couldn't believe it; Dante said he got the money from his grandma.

The pendant never left his neck. It had become integral to him now, so that each day he could make choices that he knew he needed to make. Reflecting the bad stuff, and trying to create the good stuff.

Before he went back to Fern Hill he drove to Tacoma's South End. There was a notorious house there, a big ugly white thing. It was known for its vacancy, which meant it was known for being a place to throw big parties. Or just to sit inside its bones and do not terribly healthy things.

Dante had made it beautiful. He took the idea from Marisol, and with his pendant, he was able to do something similar. It had a fresh coat of paint. The windows weren't as ragged as before, with fewer holes and a healthier look. He put out a Welcome Mat.

Once he parked the car, he clasped the pendant, then found a bouquet of roses in the passenger seat. He walked toward the house. On the fence there was a gold plaque that read:

"Martha McCormick 2002—2018. She loved life and the outdoors. She was always there for her friends. And she is loved so much by her mother, father, and brother."

Below it there were some ribbons from awards that she won in high school, 4-H and photography, and a few withering flowers. Dante cleaned it all up and lay the roses there. They were a fantastic white, to match the house.

His dad was home by the time he beat traffic. They hugged and talked about the ups and downs of the day, the funny things that happened and the sad things that happened. Dante told them that they'd be glad to know he had left fresh flowers for Martha.

"Thanks Dante," Belinda said. "You're a good brother."

"Ya know," Anton said. "Though I'd whup ya if you ever took off on us like that again, that hippy Oregon air did do wonders for you, Dante."

Dante snorted as he laughed, water almost spewing from his nose.

"Thanks, dad," Dante said. "Washington wasn't hippy enough—I had to go *into* the forest."

King Karrabad's voice didn't bother Dante anymore. He was glad to have the creepy thing gone. Focusing on what he wanted, and how he could make an impact, was easier than ever.

And in a way, he could thank the King for that.

Chapter 31

"THERAPY, SWEETIE," NADINE CALLED to her daughter.

"I know, I know," Geraldine called. "Don't have a cow, man!"

Geraldine came out from her room. The same sandy blonde hair was getting to be almost past her ears, but her blue eyes were the same as ever. She wore some mascara to make them pop.

"Nice Simpsons reference, Gerry," she said. "Let's take the Prius."

"Dad's most royal chariot? Sounds sketchy, Mom."

"I think we'll be okay this one time."

In the few months she had been back, Eugene had become a bit harder to live in.

But she was so much happier. There were times that were hard, harder than she'd really thought things could ever be, but she was glad. She had gotten a chance to look at herself honestly and found that she had been uncomfortable for a long time.

Comprehensive Mental Health was only a mile or two away, but in the evening Geraldine told her mom it was okay if she wanted to drive her. She felt much safer that way.

"I'll see you at 7:55," her mom said.

"And not a minute sooner," Geraldine winked.

Dr. Everheart was a really nice man. He appreciated Geraldine's seemingly abrupt and sudden change of identity and interests. It could be a phase, he would say, but it really doesn't matter if it is or if it isn't. You need to be happy and healthy, Geraldine, he would always say.

And he appreciated Geraldine's newfound love for antiques and tarot cards. The spy glass had often come up in their conversations.

"Having a totem to ground you in the world can be very healthy," he would say. "Have you seen Inception?"

The freedom was liberating. Having the chance to truly laugh and talk with her parents sure beat the heck out of lacrosse and ASB campaigns. To walk around the neighborhood in *her* skin, not someone else's. The strings to her marionette were cut; she was no longer nobody's monkey.

The Prius was waiting, humming its silent hum.

"I was going to go get us a tank of gas," Nadine said. "But it's like this thing is *always* full of gas."

"I guess it really *is* saving the world," Geraldine said. She clutched her spy glass.

Back at her house she looked out the window with her spy glass. Her dad knocked on the door and came in.

"What are you doing, Gerry?"

"I thought if I tried hard enough, I could see the Deschutes Forest."

"Any luck?"

"None yet," Geraldine said. "I miss my friends."

"I wonder how they're doing. Don't you keep in touch online?"

"A little bit, but they're both a lot older than me. It's only a few years, but their lives are pretty different."

"I wonder," her dad said. "Let me work on something with Mom. We'll see what we can whip up."

Geraldine read Goosebumps and dozed. A text *bzzed* on her phone.

> Toby: Hey cutie
>
> Geraldine: Hey Toby, what are you up to?
>
> Toby: Thinking about you.
>
> Geraldine: You can't just be doing that, Toby. What ELSE are you doing?
>
> Toby: Oh. Playing with my dog. It's a labradoodle.
>
> Geraldine: Aw, I love labradoodles! I knew one named Tiger and another one named Lilly.
>
> Toby: That's awesome. Want to hang out soon?
>
> Geraldine: I'll ask my parents.
>
> Toby: Cool let me know.
>
> Geraldine: <3
>
> Toby: <3

Geraldine put her phone on her desk and smiled, flopping over in her bed. It was much better to be in Eugene now. The world seemed to move over, rolling into newness, at the same moment it did in Brewer's Yawn—a seismic shift across the whole state. An awakening for Jerrold.

Chapter 32

MRS. NEUSCHWANDER'S NAME HAD been cleared. No one really knew how it happened, but all of the stuff about Mr. Dackerson online had been changed. The articles and news stories were written different—it was like Mrs. N had been right the whole time. Not a bit of slander remained on Google.

Her room had become quite the hangout since then. When parents would drop their kids off at school they would take the chance to go say hello to Mrs. Neuschwander, to commend her for her bravery and for her will. She was of course flattered, but she just folded her arms and said thank you.

All the kids would hang out in her room in the morning. White kids, Brown kids, Black kids, rich kids, poor kids—it was a veritable melting pot. Some kids would play with yo-yos and kendamas, and some would just sit and text. But it was the art room where kids really wanted to be.

"Good morning, Marisol," Mrs. Neuschwander said as the only Puentes daughter walked in. She left her conversation with the two admiring mothers in order to give Marisol a big hug.

"Buenas dias, Mrs. N," Marisol smiled.

"Feel free to get started. The clay is in the back."

Marisol relished these little moments, because she was the one who had made them possible. The dagger seemed to be more specific than the sword, and far less taxing. With her talents for pottery and coding in mind, she could create such direct and necessary changes.

"Hey."

A boy Marisol had never seen at school walked up to her out of absolutely nowhere. She was just beginning to mold the clay into a dragon. He wore a trucker hat and had stained blue jeans loosely hanging around his legs. He sported a too-adult looking leather jacket.

"Hello."

"I'm sorry I wrote that thing," the kid said. "The beaner thing."

Marisol paused. She clutched the dagger in her pocket. Then she cleared her mind, and she smiled.

"I am, too," she said. "It was stupid, and mean."

"I didn't realize what I was writing, really," he mumbled.

"Why are you apologizing now?"

"It was eating me up! I didn't smash your flowers though. That was some other kids."

"I see. Well I don't want to be your friend or anything."

"Okay," he turned away.

"I forgive you, though," she said.

He turned back and looked at her. A slow smile formed on his trembling lips.

"Thanks," he said.

Then he tipped his hat like he really was a trucker and left the room.

She turned back to her clay. When she wet her hands it was easier to mold, but so much messier. The dagger helped for things like that—clean up, take down, speeding up the kiln.

Her limit had been reached two months ago, but these days she had a lot of patience. Coding with Mr. Balzoni was even better than before. She was the best in her class, and she still had her fourth period with Mrs. N. In her language arts classes, she had started telling the teacher that learning about only White people was really starting to get old, and one girl "whoop whoop'd" her from the back of the room.

The Toyota pulled up in front of Baldwin High and she hopped in the bed. Some things never change, but Marisol enjoyed those things more than ever. It was a Friday, and seeing her familia show up was like a Christmas tree full of fat presents.

Marisol hopped out of the truck at the same familiar intersection, the corner lined with barrels of pleasant vegetables.

"Mary-soul!" Bob called out.

"It's *Marisol*, Bob. You need to learn my name!" Marisol said, love in her smile.

Bob threw a hand to his mouth to cover his embarrassment. He still smelled a bit like hand-rolled cigarettes.

"Ah shucks, Marisol. I'm sorry—you're right, you're right. I had no idea!"

"Now you do," she smiled. "I just wanted to work a little bit in the planters if I could. I have a tomato plant that needs re-potting."

They walked through the hall, big photos of Malala and Tupac watching over them. Bob helped her carry a planter to the front, and she threw on her signature yellow leather gloves.

"Oh, of course. We gonna have the pleasure of your company for long today?"

"No, I've gotta be home fairly soon."

"Then have at it, kiddo."

She dug in the planters out front. Her fingers turned the earth like it were clay. Her fingers turned the earth like her mother's and her's before that. Tomas ran by only a few moments later.

"Hermana," Tomas gasped for air. He had been running, of course.

"Hola Tomas, como estas?"

"I can't wait for the party tonight," he said. "But I have to go now. I have to go drawing."

"You have to *go* drawing?"

"The crayons need me, Marisol!" he sprinted back inside just as fast as he had run out to see her, like a confused race car.

With only a half-hour until her cousins would show up, she plunged into her gardening. Marisol loved making flowers more than ever. When the Toyota showed up in front, she brought her gloves back and collected the rambling Tomas.

Their front yard was full of petunias and poppies. They lined the walk to the freshly painted front door—a brilliant pink. Tomas exploded into the house before Marisol.

"Marisol," her mom threw her arms open. "Mija, how was it today?"

"Really good, Mom," she smiled. "A boy who had been mean to me apologized. It felt really good to hear it."

"Excellente! Well all the more reason to celebrate," she said. "Everyone's in the back already. Will you take the picadillo out, por favor?"

The backyard was alive with Puentes. Big yellow, pink, and red banners were all around the yard, draped over arborvitae and sunflowers like wedding laurels. A long white table was covered with conchas, empanadas, orejas, and arroz. Tomas brought out a big plate of sizzling tinga, the saucer bigger than his head.

Her tio Carlo had made it to Oakland just last week. Each of the cousins who had been out on their way to California had made it—one of the dagger's many helpful tricks to design paths in the world. She would sit in her room and etch what she wanted into the air, and the artifact gave it to her. She couldn't raise playgrounds out of the dirt, but she could help people get a little closer.

"Mijita," Santos called with a laugh. He walked over to Marisol and gave her a tremendous hug. "Is my brother here yet?"

Her father had quit getting together with his guy friends some time ago. Well, he still hung out with his friends, but they went and held signs outside the post office now. Marisol was pretty sure they just got together and drank too much beer before anyways, so she was glad her mom had talked some sense into him. Or maybe it had been her and the dagger's help—who could say?

"Not yet," Marisol said. "I can't wait to see Alejandra! I hope she has a good time."

Her mother burst out of the house carrying even more plates and bowls full of mouth-watering delights.

"It's *her* quinceanera isn't it? She had better enjoy it, my dear!" Lutecia laughed.

The party was the perfect start to Summer. Almost twenty Puentes were in attendance, and Alejandra truly loved her new dress, and of course she loved her cake, a traditional tres leches recipe. They listened to all kinds of music and were thick in each other's love. But Marisol dashed inside around 9 o'clock. Her laptop was already on her top bunk, and she flung open the lid. She fired up Skype.

"Hey," Rodrigo said. "How was the quinceanera?"

"Muy Buena, tan Hermosa," she gushed. "Mi prima tenias miedo de osos cuando era una niña aunque ahora que ella es una mujere mi tio compre un oso muneca por ella. Tan comico."

"That's awesome! I love how together your family is."

"It's pretty cool," she sighed. "But como estas?"

They talked a lot these days. She was teaching him how to code, and he was telling her all about the hikes they could go on when she gets back to Bend.

Epilogue

SOMETIMES IT FEELS LIKE one finds themselves in an entirely new world. A place through a thick cloud of fog, hanging low, that someone has just come to their senses and realized they entered at some point long before. More visceral than coming to in a dream, real like the humidity of a jungle dripping down your forehead.

Dante sent out the group text that began the unrolling of the fog.

> Dante: I know it's been a while, but I think we should get together one more time.

As the read receipts rolled in, they all sent texts saying they would go. When they left Oregon all those years ago, they were sure that they would meet again soon. But as is often the way with dreaming, it had never happened. The reality of their realized skills had been enough to keep their lives spry with momentum. Going backward, back to those woods and to that place, had in the end become nothing but a memory.

Mr. McCormick walked into the administrative office of Tacoma Narrows. He scratched his thick beard and smiled at the older woman behind the desk.

"Ms. Lanzig," Dante said. "I regret to say I've got to take next week off. Mind helping me draft a newsletter for my little vacay?"

"I could see to that, Mr. McCormick. I think Manny is going to be the most broken up about it."

"Manny Rodriguez?" he leaned across the desk. "I was hoping *you* might be the most broken up about it."

She gave him a peck on the lips. They looked into each others' eyes, smiling.

"I'll miss you so much," Dante told her.

"I'll miss you too, baby," she said. "Where are you running off to?"

He let her know about his reunion of sorts in Bend. She said that she was glad that he was revisiting those days, and she'd call him that night. He walked down the long hall to his office, the posters of D.A.R.E. put-me-ups and cats hanging on trees lining the walls. After shoving his laptop and "The New Jim Crow" in his bag, he buttoned up his coat and locked the door behind him.

On his way back to Fern Hill he drove by Martha's Memorial. It had become a local relic for all the families dealing with the opioid epidemic. He always used the pendant to generate a fresh bouquet of flowers. Then another to take to his mom and dad, and another to leave on his kitchen table for Ms. Lanzig.

At home he kicked off his simple shoes and stretched on the couch. He thought for a second, then wrote out one more text:

Bring your parts of the sword.

Geraldine Manderson sat on the couch. "Comedians in Cars Getting Coffee" didn't have enough episodes, she decided. *I might have to make some of those*, she thought.

After coordinating when they would meet up at The Ore-gone-ian, Geraldine put her phone down and fired up her MacBook. The silver companion's screen lit directly to her Google Drive. All her shared files and spreadsheets whirled open.

As the pages refreshed, Geraldine got up and walked into the kitchen. She staggered with each step—her hormone medication made her hips sore, and she wasn't much for needles. She had never been happier, though.

The oven's alarm dinged right as she opened the oven door, just as she hoped it would. Her oven-mitted hands took the tray out of the oven, and she dropped the sheet on the burners. The warm smell of thick peanut butter cookies layered the apartment.

"Hey, honey," Toby said as he came in the apartment.

"Hey Tobes. Cookies."

Their cat Flenderson entered the room before her husband, his poofy gray fur nuzzling against her calf. The Office had been their first big Netflix binge. Plus, how could Geraldine *not* make fun of Toby's name?

"Yum yum yum," he walked into the room. He wore his salmon pink tie that matched the thin stripes on his pinstripe shirt. He sort of wore whatever he wanted—social work was forgiving that way.

He kissed her like it was the first time. Just like he did each time. She smiled and slid her arms behind his head.

"You taste like kombucha," she said.

"It's Oregon. I'm doing the best I can. Cookie me?"

She fed him one of Shanna's most important impacts upon the world. They caught up about their day, about all the ups and downs of the things they cared about and the things they didn't. Their two big chairs for catching up were from the Recycle Store; both were less than pristine, but for them they were just right. Toby asked how she felt today.

"It's been okay," she said. "I'm definitely sore. But I got a lot done with the team in LA today. Counters my soreness."

"So amazing that Netflix lets you work remotely," Toby said. "*You* got lucky."

"*We* got lucky. Not many young couples seem to have things put together as well as we do."

"I'll count our blessings as –"

"Oh I have to go to Bend next week by the way."

Toby stopped quipping.

"Oh," he said. "For what?"

"Remember when I was fourteen?"

"And you were playing hard to get?"

"Lawl. Yes. When I first met Dante and Marisol."

Toby stood up to get more cookies. He called from the kitchen:

"Alright, no problem. Less airplane mode than that time though, yeah?"

Geraldine nodded and turned back to her computer. She fired off the emails that she needed to fire off, she edited the advertisements for next week's lineup, then she went and laid in bed. Toby sat with her in bed as he read OutdoorsNW Magazine, and she fell asleep nestled against him.

Her spyglass sat on her night table, just next to their bed.

Rodrigo opened the store in Jack London square like he did each morning—flipping the sign, unlocking the door, and rolling the ceramics cart out to the sunny Oakland sidewalk.

Each beautiful flower was painted in a gorgeous gloss. The California sun hit the earthen jewels in just the right spot, each morning. They drew an artistic eye to the otherwise commercial building.

"Buenas dias, Rodrigo!" a chipper voice called out.

Lanky and goofy Tomas rushed to the door, his feet clipping against each other as his body tried to figure out the sudden growth it was experiencing.

"Hola Tomas," Rodrigo peered beyond the high schooler. "Is Carlo with you?"

"Yeah, he drove," Tomas smiled. "I still don't have my license."

"Come on in, amigo," Rodrigo smiled back.

The inside of the store was like Wonka's factory, if it were full of computers and canvases rather than Augustus Gloop eating nougat. White plastic tables made rows in the front of the store, if you could call it that, and computers made an L along some high counters in the back. Art supplies and instructional software hung from the walls. A community bulletin was plastered with lots of advertisements for baby sitting and English lessons. In the very back there was a kiln that looked like a friendly yurt.

A white haired woman walked in the store, ringing the tiny bell. She had come by the window each morning this week, and today she decided she would make an appearance.

"Hello," she asked Rodrigo, waving a little. "Can I ask what this place is? An arts store, or a computer science thing?"

"Rigo and Mari's is all the kid's favorite spot," Rodrigo shrugged. "It's a combination of ideas. Marisol really came up with it—she calls it a hybrid maker's space. Her family was planning on the taco truck to taqueria route, which is a dope one, but when she told them what she could do they were on board."

"Plus the grant she got from some nonprofit in Washington," Carlo added, filing away bills behind the desk.

The woman's eyes went wide as she nodded her head, taking in the surroundings.

"I'll make sure and tell my grandson," she said. "He loves LEGOs, but he really loves watercolors, too!"

Mrs. Rozenberg came into the store at precisely 10 a.m. At 26-years-old she was a business owner and youth activist. Her pregnant belly meant she would be a mom soon, too.

"Marisol, you don't have to come in. You're due in a month!" Rodrigo said, throwing his hands up. He crossed the store and gave his wife a hug.

"Yo se, Rigo. I *want* to come in," she said. "Buenas dias, Carlo. Buenas dias, Tomas."

They both waved, Tomas running over to give a distended hug, before getting back to cleaning the tables. Marisol tugged Rodrigo toward the kiln in the back of the store. Then she folded her arms and looked him in the eyes.

"I have to go to Bend next week."

"A reunion, huh?" Rodrigo said, "And you're going alone?"

"I think I have to," Marisol said. "It's hard to explain, but that's how it was the first time. The other two think that's the best choice, too."

Rodrigo threw his hands on his hips and exhaled. He looked like an overworked train conductor.

"I'll hold it down," he said. "But no airplane mode on *this* trip, okay?"

Marisol kissed him. He grinned.

"Okay," she said. "Now let's get started on setting up for the 'Python and Pottery Power Hour.'"

Marisol didn't take a Bolt bus, but she did have a stop in Portland. As did Dante, since both flew. Geraldine was the only one who went by wheels, driving the old family Prius. She had offered to pick them up at the airport, but they told her it was alright to just head straight to the old cafe.

It was in the same old spot, with the zany sign hanging over head, but there was no one buzzing inside or out. Any fish swimming around these parts had stopped swimming a while back.

By no coincidence, of course, both Marisol and Dante arrived at the exact same time. Both of their drivers honked their beeping horns at the same time, then sped away. Geraldine stepped outside, zipping her blue Star Wars hoodie all the way up to her chin.

Outside The Ore-gone-ian, they saw each other for the first time in ten years. It was that foggy, odd feeling of fantasy, of seeing through the mist.

It had been a long time before they visited again, and they hadn't made the one-year reunion. Life had gotten in the way.

Marisol was pregnant. Dante had a beard and a briefcase. Jerrold was now Geraldine. There was no other way to describe the mixed feelings of disbelief and utmost joy.

"Jerry!" Dante yelled.

"Dante," Geraldine said. "You look *so* much older."

"Oh thanks," Dante said. "You look great, too. And Marisol!"

He spun and hugged her right on the spot. Marisol smiled and hugged him back as Geraldine came down from the shuttered door to the sidewalk.

"I'm glad we met here," Geraldine said. "What a rush after all this time." She paused, pointed at their surroundings and cocked her head a bit, "But it's pretty dead."

"It shut down," Marisol said, wrapping her red cardigan around herself. "Howard called me a few years ago. They're out at Casa de Shannibald. They're running a doggie daycare. And they have a grandson out there with them!"

"That's wonderful," Dante said. "It'd be good to see them, but –"

"It's kind of like last time," Marisol said. "Isn't it? They're not supposed to be involved in this part."

"No, you're right," Dante nodded. "I felt it. It wants it this way."

They walked to the back fence and peaked through the slats to see the patio, the place where they first learned about the sword. It was a different scene now—a cleared out gravel lot. But they saw themselves sitting and talking to Howard, his bristly mustache freaking them out the first time. It was like that moment was spinning at the exact same time that they looked through the fence.

Geraldine showed them to her dad's favorite chariot, and they packed all their bags inside the spacious trunk. They chattered like people who haven't seen each other in ten years do—a lot, non-stop.

They pulled up to their rental. It reminded them of Casa de Shannibald, but more urban. Inside the city limits, and very much dog-less, the unit was covered in vines and big shrubs that had been grown in their pots for a long time. She unpacked and put out a six pack of Deschutes Brewing Company beer.

Geraldine and Dante were careful not to bump or exhaust Marisol, but she was defiant. Rather than beer, she took Jasmine tea. Caffeine free.

Dante shrugged off his chestnut brown blazer and set it on the back of a seemingly brand new chair. He sat and leaned back, looking around the AirBnB rental. The couch Geraldine'd be sleeping on was smaller than the one at Casa de Shannibald, but his air mattress looked about as comfortable.

"It's good we can come together and do this," he said. "It's gotta happen. We might a' waited too long."

"I think it's alright," Marisol said. She sat down with her steaming tea. "We were using our pieces, weren't we?"

"The sword definitely gave me the power that I was looking for when I first left Eugene," Geraldine said. "I never had to go to another stupid lacrosse practice."

"It sure didn't hurt, all these years. Tacoma Narrows definitely benefitted from a few pushes in the right direction, courtesy of my pendant."

"I literally couldn't have started Rigo and Mari's without your foundation! I hardly even realized it was you that ran Tacoma Narrows when I applied for that grant."

"I've grown up a great deal, I guess," Dante said. "I'm pretty happy."

"Me too," Geraldine sighed. "Toby and I got married so young, and I was so scared, but we had so much support. Of course it's been hard, and he's been so patient with me about my transition, but we're really happy, too. I'm a real homebody, I found out."

"Do you still see things like you did in the Yawn?"

"Not really," Geraldine said. "I think it was some latent psionic thing, a Karrabad thing."

"I can't complain at *all*. Rodrigo has been a wonderful addition to the Puentes clan, and he's helped me make my business a reality. All my family members are thriving, and a ton of them work for me! My family really understands that we're a matriarchy now."

They clinked their drinks, two Oregon craft beers and one Jasmine tea. The lamp light in the room doused them all in relaxation.

"That's why I think we have to get rid of the sword for good," Dante said.

"I had a hunch, I did," Geraldine said.

"You think so, Dante?" Marisol asked. She stood up to get more hot water for her tea.

"Yeah, I do," he said. "You both know what Coyote said about it having a mind of its own. I just don't think it's smart to keep pushing it. Especially if we don't even need them anymore."

"Take the training wheels off," Geraldine nodded. "Alright alright alright."

Marisol sat down and reached in her purse for the dagger. She laid it on the table, and the other two did the same with their shards of the weapon.

"What do you suggest?" Marisol asked.

"I think we should go to the museum and talk to Benjamin," Dante said.

"A 'return it to the people' kind of thing? Sort of a weak plot line, Dante," Geraldine winked.

Dante smiled and took a drink. They agreed to go see him the first thing tomorrow.

The museum was looking better than ever. The front window and the front door were, of course, completely repaired, and had been updated to look slick and modern. And there wasn't a kobold in sight.

They found Benjamin still working on his snack bars.

"It's peanut butter protein," he mumbled through the almonds and glucose syrup. "High in good stuff, low in bad stuff, high in tasty stuff too, I should add."

"That's excellent, Benjamin," Marisol said. She folded her arms. Dante and Geraldine shared a smile.

He looked like he hadn't aged a day in the ten years since they'd last seen him selling tickets and offering unsolicited information at the front counter. Benjamin tossed a wrapper somewhere behind the register, squinting his eyes in Marisol's direction.

"Don't *sound* excellent. What do you need, hm?"

"We were hoping to see the artifacts section," Geraldine piped up.

"It'll be twenty bucks for a group rate," he said. "But I'd show ya. We've got no new exhibits or anything like that. Given all a that, I can tell ya a lot about Klamath weapons 'n such."

"That'd be great," Dante said. "Here's thirty."

The three followed the detestable guide through the museum and up the stairs, as they had when they were younger. The smell of the museum was the same, a faint whiff of tobacco laying on top of Rug Doctor. Stacks of photos and letters still reined on either side.

"Do you remember us?"

"'Course I do. Do I look daft?"

Marisol ignored his sass just like she did as a kid. She was less insecure than she used to be, and better all the time.

"You don't look daft. You look exactly the same as you used to."

Benjamin rested his arm on the case, the whole thing well repaired since their last visit to the rectangular room. In the case, like it had always been there, was a stand. It was a handsome wooden stand that looked like it could hold a Winchester or some other long arm. But of course it wasn't built for that.

"You haven't changed at all, girlie," Benjamin said, a long smile spreading on his face. "You three didn't find a spot for the sword then, heh?"

"We've been using it, in little ways," Geraldine said. "But we don't need it anymore."

"And it never wanted to be with us, did it?" Dante asked.

Coyote shrugged. He was in his full anthropomorphic form again. Ten years later he still towered over the three fishies.

"Who can say," Coyote said. "It's hard enough to understand where *I* fit into this new world. The sword probably took a liking to you."

"Or something like that," Marisol said. "But we had a better idea."

Coyote raised one lupine eyebrow.

"Don't pretend you didn't have the same one," she said, folding her arms. "There's already a place for it to be displayed."

"Okay," Coyote grinned again. "Fair's fair. My people could stand for a little inspiration, a little empowerment to make their own decisions, their own impact. I think the sword gets that, too."

Marisol took the dagger out of her purse. Geraldine brought out her spyglass, and Dante unslung the pendant from around his neck. They stood in a triangle and each of them felt that old whip of wind and crackle of light. The pieces of the sword lit up with that pink glow, then rose toward each other in the air. They swirled and collected themselves, old friends rekindling. The pieces combined into their familiar, unitary shape.

The sword sank slowly into Marisol's outstretched hands. It looked just like it did that day that they had found it in Brewer's Yawn—sterling and austere.

She stepped toward the case and extended the weapon to Coyote. He took it in his paws.

"Jeeze, I sure don't want to handle this thing any longer than I have to," he said. "Once it's in the case, it'll stay there for a long time. Hopefully it'll be happier here than in a well, or split into three pieces along the coast."

"I think it will be," Geraldine said. "Call it a remnant of the sight it gave me ten years ago."

All four walked to the front of the Cultural Center, and, though they had expected that they would talk to Coyote about his adventures and his life, they hardly spoke at all. It was like attending a wake; it was a celebration, but it was also clearly a loss.

"Kalapuyans and colonists alike, and all their descendants, will now be able to gain the same empowerment that you three did. Just by visiting the sword," Coyote said. "No one speaks our language anymore. But we still hold onto the culture of our elders.

He paused and looked at them all, taking each in with his big eyes.

"Ten years later and you kids still inspire me."

"Aw shucks, Coyote," Geraldine said. "You're just saying that."

"I meant it then and I mean it now," he grinned. "You're just as modest as I remember you, Geraldine."

Dante gave Coyote a hug. They were all a little taken aback, but as Coyote leaned into the hug, Marisol and Geraldine joined on either side. In those quiet moments, they were able to find their familiarity.

They walked out of the Cultural Center and onto the main drag. There was a palpable absence of their pieces of the sword, but they each had been waiting for it for a long time, and each one knew that it was right. It was a heavy recognition, but a recognition all the same, that they could now make all the changes that they needed, all on their own.

Marisol ordered a Lyft to return to the AirBnB. They laughed, remembering just how many Lyfts they had to take during their original visit. Their driver was no miffed college graduate or angry political fanatic. It was, in fact, a quiet drive.

Each began to pack their bags as soon as they walked into the flat; they hadn't talked about the time to head out, but it was clear. As they packed, Dante played John Denver from his phone.

"You *dog*, Dante!" Geraldine said.

Dante said he had to, and Marisol laughed.

All three of them had gained a lot that week in Central Oregon a decade ago. The Deschutes Forest had given them so much. Time to heal, time to strengthen, and time to evolve. They each made two life-long friends. And they each took home new tools, physical and emotional, to make change in their lives every day.

Coyote still walks throughout the hills and the forests of Oregon, and the boqs are still free to breathe the wonderful arboreal air. Not as many people as they would like treat them with the respect they deserve—who else is going to take care of the woods and the rivers while everyone else is inside watching Netflix?

But they loved their adventures with the three fishies from the West Coast. If they come back for good someday, they'll make sure to throw them a party that even Amhuluk could enjoy. For now, though, the three travelers, the two café owners, the one native leader, and all those boqs and kobolds, will just have to keep making a difference in their own lives each and every day.

www.ingramcontent.com/pod-product-compliance
Lightning Source LLC
Chambersburg PA
CBHW051139020726
47501CB00005B/1580